Waiting To Score

Elouise Tynan

This is a work of fiction. All the characters, organisations, and events portrayed in the novel are either productions of the author's imagination or are used fictitiously.

WAITING TO SCORE

Edited: Amy Maranville at Kraken Communications
Cover design: Sarah Paige at Opium House Creatives
Cover image: Michelle Lancaster @lanefotograf
Cover model: Andy Murray

Published by Ardently Romance

Ebook: 978-0-6453768-0-7
Paperback: 978-0-6453768-1-4

 Created with Vellum

To my parents, for teaching me how to write.
To my husband, for supporting me while I write.
To my son, for loving me while I write.

And to me, for writing it.
I knew you could do it.

Chapter One

MONTY

I slid my hand into his before I knew what I was doing. His palm was warm and solid and unexpectedly large.

I dared a glance over my shoulder searching for that mop of dirty blond hair I didn't want to see coming through the crowd.

"Can I help you?" the guy beside me asked, glancing down at our joined hands, then at me.

I turned to face him, my eyebrows shooting up my forehead.

He was *stupidly* hot. Straight nose, light brown hair, and striking blue eyes surrounded by dark lashes that would be the envy of any woman. And that jaw. That jaw put sharp-cut diamonds to shame.

"I...um..."

I was suddenly finding it hard to remember why I was holding hands with a guy who looked like he'd stepped off the set of *Riverdale*.

"Oh, I can't wait to hear this," one of Hot Guy's friends said, his eyes shining with humor. All three of them waited, clearly expecting an explanation for why I'd attached myself to a random guy on the quad. In my defense, I didn't know he was so damn hot. His hand had been the closest in my time of need, so I'd taken it.

Hot Guy tried to pull away just as the very face I didn't want to see appeared through the crowd of students gathered on the quad.

"Wait!" I gripped his arm to stop him. "Pretend to be my boyfriend. I'll pay you."

He looked at me like I'd just offered to blow him with a mouthful of herpes. Which to be fair, I could kind of understand. Not because I had mouth herpes. But who grabbed a total stranger and begged them to play pretend couple? As far as first impressions went, this one was insane.

"I don't need your money," he said, frowning down at me.

Holy shit, he was tall. Had he been this tall ten seconds ago or was it just the irritation starting to cloud his face that made him more imposing?

"Please? Just do me this favor and I'll give you whatever you want." I gave him what I hoped was my most pleading and innocent smile.

"Oh, this just keeps getting better and better," his friend said, both his buddies trying and failing to hold in their laughter.

A glance in my periphery showed that mop of dirty blond hair closing in.

"Are you for real right now?" Hot Guy asked, eyes darting around the quad. "Do we know each other? Did Davis put you up to this?"

He ran his free hand—the one not currently taken

hostage by me—through his hair, the muscles of his bicep flexing to show off a seriously toned arm.

My gaze snagged on his clothes, eyes running over him and his two friends. They were all dressed the same—Nike sneakers, navy sweat shorts and a navy Pierson University basketball t-shirt.

Basketball players, damn it. Didn't this just kept getting better and better?

I'd thoroughly humiliated myself in front of some of the most wanted guys on campus. I'd have to make time to be embarrassed later. Right now, I was desperate. And I was out of time.

"This isn't a joke. I swear I'm not crazy, I just need your help."

Hot Guy's eyes roamed my face, taking up seconds I didn't have, which meant I was about to do something that would solidify me as the most bat-shit girl these guys had ever accidentally encountered.

"I'm so sorry in advance for this."

A question formed in Hot Guy's eyes, but he didn't get a chance to ask it because I gripped his face, tugging his mouth to mine. Kissing him was like kissing a stone wall of surprise, and I screwed my eyes shut, heat flooding my cheeks at my own ridiculousness.

Desperate times and all that... but it still didn't change the fact I'd jumped a perfect stranger. An incredibly *hot* stranger.

I slid my fingers through his hair and his mouth relaxed against mine, his surprise morphing into something much friendlier. His hand closed over my hip, making me squeak, his other hand sliding over my ass. My lips parted all on their own, his tongue sweeping into my mouth in lazy, practiced strokes.

God, he was a good kisser.

Scratch that, he was a phenomenal kisser. And if this kiss went on for the rest of the week, I'd die hot and happy.

"Well, that escalated quickly," one of his friends said, but I barely heard him, too wrapped up in Hot Guy's hands on my body and his tongue in my mouth.

That was, until I heard the one voice that was like a bucket of ice water down my back.

"Monty?"

I stiffened, turning my head, lips still attached to Hot Guy and his fingers still curled around my hips.

Plastering a look of surprise on my face, I reluctantly pulled my mouth away, and I could have sworn Hot Guy frowned in annoyance.

"Alec."

My dirty-blond ex-boyfriend looked me up and down, blowing out a breath. "I thought it was you. I knew you'd transferred to Pierson. I was hoping to run into you."

I turned in Hot Guy's hold so my back was to his chest, pulling his muscular arms around my waist, hoping it looked like he was holding onto me willingly.

"Well, here I am!" I said to Alec a little too brightly.

No need to overcompensate just because I'd found myself in the most awkward situation of my entire life. One of my own ridiculous making.

I hesitated for the briefest moment over the words I was about to utter. But I'd come this far. Time to shoot my shot and pray to everything that was holy Hot Guy would play along.

"I transferred here a few weeks ago to be closer to my boyfriend." I slapped a hand over Hot Guy's at my waist and smiled at him over my shoulder.

Those intense blue eyes stared down at me, making my heart pound in my chest.

Please don't out me. Please don't out me. Please don't out me.

His gaze slid to Alec, and he extended his hand. "Nice to meet you, bro. I'm West."

West. He even had a hot guy name.

Alec stared at West's offered hand then ignored it completely, his gaze cutting back to me.

"Since when do you have a boyfriend? I spoke to your mom last week, and she didn't mention it."

Shit. He had me there. Anyone who knew me at all knew I told my mom everything. Well, *almost* everything. I hadn't told her about the way Alec had been acting this past year.

"No, well..." I said, fumbling for an explanation. "We've been keeping this pretty quiet. Just between us, you know?"

Alec's gaze narrowed. "Why?"

God, his persistence was annoying. Why did he even care?

I worked to think of a lie, my mind offering up a sum total of nothing.

"Oh, um..." I bit the inside of my cheek.

West's arms tightened around my waist. "Because I'm on the basketball team."

He bent over, resting his chin on my shoulder and his cheek against mine as if he'd done it a thousand times before. I sagged against him in relief, the smell of his cologne invading my senses. He smelled incredible, had a face Taylor Swift would write songs about, and he was helping me lie to Alec. I'd really lucked out with my choice of fake boyfriend.

"So?" Alec asked, gaze finally cutting to West to size him up.

West stood tall, hands sliding off my waist to sling an arm around my shoulders and tuck me to his side. I fit perfectly beneath his arm, the two of us at just the right heights.

"The female fans can be a little crazy, man," West's buddy offered, and I shot him a grateful smile.

So grateful I could cry. They had no idea what they were saving me from.

"He's not kidding," the other friend added. "I once came home to find a naked basketball bunny in my bed inside my *locked* dorm room." He shuddered.

"I mean... you didn't have to let her blow you, dude. You could have kicked her out," the first one said, the corners of his mouth twitching.

The second one shrugged, clearly perplexed at the suggestion of turning away a naked girl, even if she wasn't opposed to a little breaking and entering.

"I didn't want to subject Monty to all that, at least not right away," West said as though it were nothing and not some of the sweetest, most considerate words a college guy had probably ever uttered in defense of the random girl he'd met three minutes ago.

I tilted my head up at him with what I hoped was a look of pure adoration. It wasn't that much of a stretch at this point, given he and his friends were officially my campus knights.

"We wanted to take the time to make sure this was right before we went public and told our families." West's intense blue eyes stared down at me, his hand coming up to stroke my cheek, the touch sending a shiver skittering over my skin. "But we know that it's right. I couldn't be more into this girl."

My stomach swooped, my lusty lady parts clearly not getting the memo that we were faking it.

Alec cleared his throat, and I reluctantly pulled my gaze from West's.

"There are things we need to talk about," Alec said, back to ignoring my fake boyfriend completely. "Can we have dinner one night this week?"

I opened my mouth to reply, mind scrolling through all the ways I could rebuff that idea without encouraging Alec any further than I somehow already had, when West cut in.

"Oh yeah, man, of course. We'd love to have dinner. Name a time and place and we'll be there. I recommend Ruby's. They do one hell of a burger."

He offered Alec a killer smile, all straight white teeth and shining blue eyes, and I bit my lip to stifle my laugh.

"Sure, whatever," Alec said tightly, his eyes never leaving me. "I'll text you, Monty."

Please don't, I thought as Alec turned to go.

"Nice to meet you, bro. Looking forward to that catch up," West called.

Alec slipped through the crowd on the quad, throwing a look over his shoulder.

West smiled broadly, raising a hand to wave, but I grabbed his wrist, pulling it down and swinging out from under him.

He raised an eyebrow at me in question.

"So, about that..." I said, heat creeping into my cheeks.

"Girl, that was some of the best shit I've seen all week!" West's friend said, throwing his head back with a laugh.

"Did you clock West's face when she kissed him?" the other asked.

7

West's glare shut them both up.

"Friend of yours?" he asked me.

"Ex."

"I figured. Care to give me a little more info about why you just sucked my face off in front of him?"

I screwed up my face. "Excuse me, that kiss was some of my best work. It's not my fault kissing you was like making out with one of the marble statues outside the library."

His eyebrows shot up.

"Oh, she didn't," West's teammate said, bending over to press his hands to his knees.

"She did," the other one said, looking awed. "She just compared the King of Campus to a stone statue."

West's jaw clenched. "Don't you two have somewhere else to be?"

"We don't, actually."

"Find somewhere," West said.

Shooting me broad grins, they strolled away, not bothering to cover their laughter, which filtered back to us through the busy quad.

I crossed my arms over my chest. "King of Campus, huh? That's quite a title."

He shrugged. "It's the basketball jersey they want."

"Are you the captain?"

"Hell no."

"Just the team stud?"

"Yeah. I mean, no." He looked momentarily flustered, and I tried not to laugh. "This isn't about me."

"Maybe it should be," I said as my phone buzzed in my pocket. I pulled it out to read a text from my friend Stella, speaking absently to West. "Your story sounds a hell of a lot more interesting than mine."

He crossed his impressive arms over his even more

impressive chest, those blue eyes scanning me and making my stomach twist in the best way. "I'd rather hear yours."

"And it's a story I'd love to tell you," I said, shoving my phone back in the pocket of my denim cut-offs. "But I have to go."

"Are you serious?"

I screwed up my nose and pointed at my pocket. "Emergency SOS text, I'm needed elsewhere." I backed away, edging around a nearby group of students. "But thank you. You really helped me out of a jam. You're a prince and a gentleman and all those other great things men hope to be."

"Monty..."

The sound of my name coming from his mouth was something else.

"I'm sorry!" I called. "I absolutely owe you one!"

He shook his head in disbelief, and I jogged down the path, thanking the college Gods for delivering me such a perfect boy to accost in my time of need.

Maybe this new school was going to be fun after all.

Chapter Two

WEST

I'd spent three days looking out for the little rocket with legs for days who'd jumped me in the quad, zeroing in on every brunette I caught on campus.

So when I spotted her leaving one of the dining halls, I jogged up at her side. She had her head bowed, staring down at her phone, walking toward the arts and social sciences quad.

I slung an arm around her shoulders, her eyes widening in surprise.

"West," she said, sliding her phone in the pocket of her tight jeans and crossing her arms over her incredible tits. I couldn't help but notice her stellar body, especially all the parts that had been pressed against me when we'd kissed.

"Do you make a habit of surprising girls on their way to class?" she asked, those wide grey-blue eyes meeting mine.

I'd been hoping to run into her again, maybe score her number. I didn't do relationships, even fake ones, but damn if I didn't love the way her lips had felt on mine and the way her perfect ass fit in my hands. I'd spent the past three days thinking of ways I could do it again. I wanted to spend more time with her—preferably in my bed—which meant I had to turn on the charm.

"You really think you're one to talk when it comes to surprising people?"

She pulled a face that was a cross between a cringe and a nod of agreement. "You've got me there. But in my defense, I was desperate."

I cut a sideways glance at her. "Desperate to taste my tongue."

She shoved at my chest, and I chuckled. But instead of pulling away like I expected, her arm came around my waist to steady herself as we strolled along the arched walkway.

"Don't worry, you can tell me," I teased. Or was it outright flirting? It came so naturally these days it was hard to tell. "You took one look at me across the quad and decided you had to have me, so you marched over and took charge. I dig a girl who knows what she wants. But you didn't have to ask that poor guy to harass you to cover your tracks."

I tried to hide my smile at her outrage.

"You're really full of yourself, you know that?"

"I do know that, actually."

We left the walkway and headed down the winding path across the lawn.

"And I didn't pay Alec to be my cover story. He's been a problem for a while now." A frown etched her face.

"What kind of problem are we talking?"

"It's a long, boring story," she said, waving me away.

"It ended, or maybe it started, with you jumping me in front of my teammates. So far I'm not bored."

She glanced up, shooting me a small smile, and the urge to dip my head and kiss her hit me full force.

Fuck, she was beautiful.

As surprised as I'd been at the time, I'd lucked out being the one she'd mauled in her time of need. And if she wanted a repeat, I'd be all too happy to oblige.

"I'm going to take a stab and say Alec isn't a happy ex?"

She sighed. "We dated for almost two years in high school and broke up right before we left for college, only Alec acted like the conversation never happened. We went to separate colleges but that didn't stop him texting or calling me, he even drove out to see me uninvited more than once."

I frowned. "So, how did you both end up here?"

"I transferred for the writing program and because my childhood best friend goes here. I was so excited when my transfer got approved for sophomore year. Only when I arrived three weeks ago, I found out Alec was here, too." She shook her head. "I never would have come if I had thought..."

We passed a couple of guys from the football team, and I nodded in greeting before turning my attention back to Monty. "Seems kind of convenient. Did he come here for you?"

She stared out over the rolling green lawn as we walked, groups of students spread out in the early fall sunshine.

"I have no idea. Maybe? I'm too afraid of what the answer might be to ask."

I stopped us both, gripping her shoulders and looking into her eyes. "This guy sounds a little intense."

Her teeth worried over her bottom lip. "I don't know. I think maybe he's just having trouble moving on? It's not like

12

he's a creep or anything. I've known him since I was in second grade."

Didn't mean he wasn't a creep, but I didn't know her well enough to say that and I didn't want to drive her away by pushing too hard. So I changed the subject.

"You going to the party on Greek Row tonight?"

"Maybe."

"I'll be there," I said, wiggling my eyebrows at her.

She backed away along the path, her eyes filled with humor. "Well, in that case, I'll pass."

I clutched my chest. "Monty, that hurts."

"I'm sure there'll be plenty of girls at the party to help you lick your wounds."

"Probably, but only one I want helping me lick anything." I gave her a pointed look.

She rolled her eyes and waved, not even breaking stride as she disappeared down the path.

Had she just outright rejected me?

Well, fuck. That was a first.

Chapter Three

MONTY

"Tell me again why we're at a frat party if you hate frat boys?" I called to Imogen over the music and taking a sip of my warm beer.

The cups had been thrust into our hands by three freshman pledges the moment we'd stepped through the door. Clearly someone had forgotten to cool the keg, a punishable offense on Greek Row.

"Because..." she said. "While it's true that frat parties include ridiculous frat jerks, they also include all football, hockey and basketball boys." She wiggled her eyebrows, and I couldn't help but laugh.

"Oh, my bad, I didn't realize we were on the hunt for an athletic future-husband for you tonight."

Her face split in a sly smile. "We're always on the hunt for that."

She knocked her cup against mine and we downed the warm beer, trying not to gag.

Imogen had been my best friend since we were in

second grade. We'd met when my family moved from Florida to Hartford for my dad's job. We'd been inseparable ever since, all the way up until graduation when she'd come to Michigan to go to Pierson, and I'd gone to Florida State. I thought I'd love the sunny weather and year-round warmth... but as it turned out, after years of Connecticut winters, the humid swampy South wasn't for me. And neither was the distance from my family or my best friend.

It didn't help that my ex-boyfriend had ended up a mere five-hour drive away at the University of Alabama. Alec had made two uninvited trips last year to "surprise" me by turning up at my dorm. I tried to remind him that we were broken up, but he brushed it off. He said that he was having trouble adjusting to college life in Alabama, and he needed me; I was the closest thing to home he had. At least, that's what he'd told me at the time.

Only that didn't explain how or why he'd ended up at Pierson this year.

Maybe it was to be closer to his aunt and uncle. His uncle was a police officer in Ann Arbor, and Alec was close with him.

My stomach twisted with discomfort at the thought of Alec's persistence that day on the quad, but I brushed it aside. This was a new year, and I was a sophomore at a new school with my best friend by my side again. Alec was irrelevant.

Pierson had an amazing writing program I still couldn't believe I'd been accepted into. It had been an added bonus that Imogen and I got to be reunited as a result. I'd moved into a dorm suite with her and her friend Stella, who she'd met at freshman orientation, and who I'd met a few times when I'd come to visit Imogen last year. Which meant she was now *our* best friend Stella, and I couldn't be more excited about my fresh start living together.

"Don't look now, but I think we're being assessed for our Pound Town potential," Imogen said, tilting her head at a group of guys to our left.

"Using the phrase 'Pound Town' is a party foul, Imogen. Do it again and I'm dragging your ass home."

She laughed, just as two of the guys broke away from their friends and threaded through the throng in our direction.

"Ladies," said the one wearing a white polo with his collar popped, giving us a megawatt smile. He was cute in that slick, country club kind of way. Not my type.

Imogen didn't seem to mind though, matching his smile and offering him a hand.

"Imogen," she said over the thumping bass of a Doja Cat song, all but batting her lashes at him.

"Stanton." Because of course that was his name.

His friend offered me a hand, his eyes subtly roaming over my bare legs in my leather miniskirt. "I'm Matt."

He was just as cute but way less pretentious than his friend in a black button-down shirt and faded jeans. His dark hair was pushed back from his clean-shaven baby face, dark brown eyes waiting for me to take his hand.

"Monty," I said, shaking it.

"Matt and Monty. We sound great together."

"You think so?" I said, humoring his attempt to flirt.

He nodded, giving me a broad smile. "I haven't seen you around before. Are you a sorority girl?"

I shook my head. "Organized sisterhoods aren't really my thing."

"Shame," he said, eyeing me over his cup as he took a sip.

The guy was sporting a boner for sorority sisters. *Noted.*

"So, what's your major?" I asked, clutching at a tried-and-true small talk question.

"Marketing. You?"

"Officially undeclared, but most likely creative writing."

Matt smiled. "You're a writer?"

"Hopefully one day."

The crowd jostled behind him, and Matt stumbled into me, using the opportunity to slide closer, his chest brushing my arm.

He was confident and with good reason. Most girls wouldn't kick him out of bed if it came down to it. But I wasn't looking for a fumbling hook-up in some guy's dorm room. That had never been my scene. Imogen was the one on the prowl tonight, I was just here to play wing woman.

Matt was leaning closer to whisper in my ear when a set of strong hands closed around my waist from behind. Before I could blink, I was spun around, and a warm mouth closed over mine.

I tried to rear back, but fingers tangled in my hair, holding me in place.

I was about to claw at the face of the jerk accosting me when his tongue swept into my mouth and lust-fueled memories clouded my mind.

I knew those lips.

I knew those arms.

I knew the hard planes of that athletic chest.

West's hand trailed down my spine, stopping just above my ass, his mouth devouring me like he was starved for human contact. Heat flared between us, and every thought I'd ever had about him became X-rated in an instant.

Holy hell, I'd forgotten how well this guy could kiss.

He pulled away with a satisfied grin.

17

"What was that?" I asked, working to catch my breath.

He leaned in, his lips brushing my ear making me shiver.

"Alec is here. I couldn't let some other guy flirt with my girl while he's watching."

"Oh... thanks, I guess?"

"Any time, babe." He slipped an arm around my waist, turning to Matt. "Thanks for keeping her company, man. I'll take it from here."

Before I had a chance to protest, West turned us around and threaded through the crowd, girls calling out to him or guys slapping him high-fives as we made our way to the kitchen.

"Did you win a game tonight or something?" I asked, as yet another person congratulated him.

"Sure did. Forty-six point steamroll!"

His face lit with the most enthused smile I'd ever seen, and my stomach flipped at the sight.

Ugh, get a grip. It's just a smile.

Every guy had one and this guy definitely knew how to work his to his advantage.

He gestured to the bottles of liquor lined up on the kitchen counter and pulled two red cups from the stack, turning them upright. "What's your poison, babe?"

I tiled my head, considering. "Three shots of tequila and an Adderall."

He looked momentarily stunned, before his expression smoothed into its usual easy smile. "You're messing with me."

I nodded. "Vodka soda would be great."

West got to work mixing the drinks, his muscles flexing through his light blue linen button-down. He'd paired it with dark jeans and brown leather loafers, looking like a male model who'd wandered off from a cover shoot and found himself at a frat party.

But just because we'd played the role of two people who were dating—twice now—didn't mean I was in a rush to get mixed up with him for real. I didn't need to know him anymore than I already did to know that anything between us wouldn't end well for me and my soft, relationship-loving heart. Just polling the girls we'd befriended on our dorm floor was enough to get a clear picture of the reputation West had no doubt enjoyed earning for himself. The guy was allergic to commitment.

"I really need to pee," I blurted out.

West's hands stilled on the vodka bottle, eyes sliding in my direction. "That's the sexiest thing any girl has ever said to me."

He nodded over his shoulder towards the hall. "Bathroom's that way. You take care of business while I finish making the drinks."

The line to the bathroom was thankfully short so I was in and out fast. Imogen accosted me as soon as I opened the door.

Gripping my arm, she tugged me into the hallway. "Did someone slip me a hallucinogen, or did I just see you making out with West Wright?"

"No, you're not high. But it's not what it looks like," I said over my shoulder as we cut through the crush of people towards the kitchen.

"Okay... so what's it like then?"

"Alec's here. He was helping me out of a jam."

Imogen blanched at the mention of my ex. "He's here? At the party?"

I grimaced. "Alec may be under the impression that West and I are dating."

Imogen stopped halfway down the hall, crossing her arms over her chest. The trio of freshman girls behind her squeaked in protest before maneuvering around us.

Imogen raised an eyebrow. "And how exactly would Alec have gotten that impression?"

I chewed on my thumbnail, knowing she was going to make a bigger deal out of it than it was.

"I may have jumped West in the quad and begged him to pretend to be my boyfriend to get rid of Alec."

Imogen's eyebrows rose so high they disappeared beneath her bangs.

"You jumped the biggest stud on the basketball team?"

I cringed at the memory and nodded.

"Jumped him, how?"

"Grabbed his face and kissed him."

Imogen's eyes widened. "Oh my God!"

"I know," I said, burying my face in my hands.

Her laughter filled the air. "You're a trip, you know that?"

She linked her arm with mine and we elbowed our way to the kitchen to find West with the same two teammates he'd been with the day on the quad.

"Quad Girl!" one called, sliding off the counter.

Imogen snorted a laugh. "Quad Girl. Sounds dirty."

I elbowed her in the ribs, turning back to him. "It's Monty, actually."

The guy chuckled. "We know, Wright's mentioned you enough."

I raised my eyebrows in West's direction. He'd talked to his friends about me?

"I've mentioned you twice. Bant needs to calm down."

"Bant?" Imogen asked.

"Luke Bantempelli," he said, offering Imogen his hand.

20

She gave him a once over, taking in his blond hair, blue eyes and the toned arms that were currently on full display in the grey Pierson Basketball t-shirt that stretched around his toned biceps. The faded ripped jeans were the icing on the tasty cake that I knew was exactly Imogen's flavor.

She took his offered hand and he brought it to his lips. "And you are?"

She stared at him as his lips touched her knuckles. "Wondering what the hell you're doing right now. Does this routine actually work on women?"

Bant dropped her hand. "Usually."

"Never," their other teammate said at the same time.

"This is Adam," West said.

Adam raised his beer in our direction, dark brown eyes smiling, his caramel-colored hair peeking out from under a backwards Pierson Basketball cap. "Everyone calls me Van."

West picked up two full cups from the counter, passing one to me and the other to Imogen.

"So, what? You're a three-man basketball team? Where's the rest of you?" Imogen asked, taking a sip of her drink and nodding at West in appreciation.

Not only was the boy a walking, talking snack and basketball stud, he made a mean cocktail as well.

"They're around," Van said with a shrug. "We can introduce you if you want."

"Oh, I want," Imogen muttered into her cup, taking another sip.

Bant's eyes narrowed on her, giving her a once over. "You're telling me you think you can find better company than the three biggest lady killers on the team?"

Imogen laughed. "Who says lady killer anymore?"

She was one to talk, given she'd used the term 'Pound

Town' earlier, but I'd let her bicker this one out with Bant. Imogen loved a good bout of verbal sparring with a willing victim.

West leaned against the counter, sipping his drink, content to watch our friends go at it and my god, I wanted to run my tongue over every inch of him.

I needed to rein it in. We'd kissed twice, we weren't about to walk down the aisle. Nor did I want to with the biggest fuckboy on the basketball team, no matter how good he looked in a pair of jeans or how phenomenally he kissed.

"I say lady killer," Bant cut back. "And you can guarantee if I'm saying it, it's going to make a big comeback."

"Wow, full of yourself much?" Imogen said.

West's gaze slid to me, calling me over with a tilt of his head. I stepped in front of him, his hand snaking around my waist to tug me closer until I was standing between his legs.

"You're very handsy tonight. Is this a thing we do now?" I said, bringing my drink to my lips to cover my smile.

I loved the feel of his hands on me, but he didn't need to know that.

He discarded his drink on the counter, skimming his other hand over my shoulder, fingers tangling in my hair. "I'm your fake boyfriend. Surely that earns me a handsy allowance?"

When I didn't answer he leaned in, our faces much closer than I would consider friendly. The thudding beat of the music in the living room matched the thudding beat of my heart and I arched my back ever so slightly, my hips pressing into his in the lightest touch.

"You're only my fake boyfriend when Alec's around, and I don't see him," I said, trying to play it cool, when inside I was fighting the urge to maul him.

West glanced at the door to the kitchen over my shoulder. "Hup, I just saw him."

A panty-melting grin spread across his face before his mouth descended on mine. There was nothing slow or lazy about our kiss this time. It was demanding and urgent and full of unchecked desire that had my stomach tightening with need. I slid my hands over the muscles of his shoulders, wrapping my arms around his neck and tilting my head to deepen the kiss, pulling a low groan from West. Both his hands slid to my lower back, tugging me against him until there wasn't an inch of space between us.

A little voice in the back of my head told me to pull away, that getting mixed up with West wasn't something I wanted to do. But there was no way I was going to pull out of a kiss this good.

"For fuck's sake, I'm not watching you two make out again," Van said, a scowl in his voice. "Get a fucking room."

I laughed against West's mouth.

"No one asked you to watch me with my girl," West replied, his eyes trained on me.

I glanced at Imogen in time to see her eyes go comically wide.

"I'm only your fake girlfriend," I reminded him.

Not that there had been anything fake about the way we'd just made out. We were practically grinding on each other in a fully-lit kitchen.

"No one needs to know about the fake part," West murmured, mouth closing over mine again.

Kissing him gave me a high, and I was quickly becoming an addict.

But I wasn't usually the kind of girl who let desire run away from me or override my better judgment. West wasn't a random college guy. He was the star of the basketball team and not even remotely my type. I didn't go for self-assured jocks who were only interested in getting in and getting off. West wasn't a commitment kind of guy, which meant he wasn't my kind of guy. I'd never been into meaningless flings and I didn't want to start now. Least of all with the campus king of casual hook-ups. And definitely not when I still had Alec to deal with. One relationship drama was enough to keep me completely occupied.

I pressed a hand to West's chest, pulling back. It almost hurt to do it, but I needed to put distance between us.

West's grip flexed on my hips. "Where are you going?"

"I think we should quit while we're ahead," I said. "Maybe, remember this isn't real."

West stared at me for a moment. "It could be," he said, a slow smile under-cutting the seriousness of his words.

I huffed in reply. "You really think I'm going to believe Mr. Anti-Commitment wants to tie himself down? And to someone he barely knows?"

West's brow creased. "Mr. Anti-Commitment?"

I shrugged. "I asked around about you."

The corner of his mouth hitched up. "And what did you find out? That I'm a god in bed? You could have just asked me, babe. I would have told you that. Or better yet, I could show you."

His hand slid over my ass, squeezing gently.

I rolled my eyes. "It was definitely entertaining hearing about all the girls you've humped and dumped. You've left quite the trail of broken hearts across campus."

"Humped and dumped?"

The humor in his expression made my chest ache. He was at least twenty five percent more attractive when he was amused. Given the guy was already off the charts in the

24

looks department, it was all I could do not to drop dead from his grin.

"I'm a total gentleman, Monty. You've clearly got me confused with someone else."

I tilted my head, pretending to mull it over. "You know, I don't think I do."

He leaned in again, my body anticipating the delicious feel of his lips on mine, when an all-too-familiar voice cut through the room.

"Monty. Can I talk to you please?"

My spine stiffened, and I glanced over my shoulder at Alec. His eyes were dark with anger.

"We're a little busy right now, man," West said, his lips brushing my throat and making me gasp.

I bit my lip, heat flooding me along with a heavy dose of guilt. I wanted Alec to take the hint and leave me alone, but this was almost cruel. He and I had cared about each other once.

"I'll be right back," I said, reluctantly slipping from West's grasp, his expression lighting with momentary surprise.

"Let's talk outside," Alec said, and he headed for the back door without waiting.

I followed, sliding the door shut behind us. A group of seniors from the football crowd were gathered on the back porch, drinking and laughing, the thumping bass of the music in the living room still audible even with the doors closed. A large bonfire burned at the bottom of the yard, surrounded by people, one of them playing a guitar.

Alec veered to the left away from everyone, heading for a cluster of half-dead rose bushes. Clearly there were no green thumbs in this frat house.

"What is it, Alec? It's cold, I want to get back inside."

I rubbed at my arms, my low-slung party top no match for the chilly fall weather.

He rounded on me. "What the hell are you doing in there?"

"Having a good time."

His eyes simmered with anger. "I mean, what the hell are you doing in there with *him*? And the other day on the quad? I know he's not your boyfriend."

"And how would you know that?"

Alec stepped closer. "Because *I* am. You need to stop messing around."

I stared at the boy I'd cared about once-upon-a-time, noting the slightly crazed look in his eyes. When he'd texted me nonstop and turned up at my dorm last year, I'd believed it when he'd said he was having trouble adjusting to college and being away from home. But something had definitely shifted. This wasn't the boy I knew, and this wasn't about being homesick or not fitting in.

Alec had always been a little possessive when we dated in high school, telling me to cover up if I wore anything as revealing as a tank top or getting angry when other guys spoke to me for too long. But the manic edge to his expression now had me taking a tentative step back.

"You and I broke up, Alec. I don't know where you got this idea in your head that I didn't mean it, but I did."

He moved closer. "Because it's bullshit. We're great together, Monty. That jock doesn't care about you. He doesn't know you, not like I do. He just wants to get in your pants."

I crossed my arms over my chest. "Well, then it's a good thing I'm wearing a skirt."

Alec's eyes flashed. "Don't joke about that. Don't even think about giving him what's mine."

I reared back. "What's yours? Nothing about me is yours, Alec. You need to move on because I'm already doing the same."

I turned to walk away but he came after me.

"Don't follow me, Alec. Stay away from me, okay?"

I headed for the steps to the back porch, taking them two at a time and hurrying back to the crowded party. I knew deep down Alec was harmless.

Surely that crawling feeling in the pit of my stomach was just the alcohol.

Chapter Four

WEST

"So, we're just supposed to believe you're wifed up now with the girl who kissed you on the quad?" Bant asked, taking a jump shot. It bounced off the ring, joining the pounding of bouncing basketballs echoing around the gym at practice.

"Sure as shit looked like they were together at the frat party," Van said, putting up a shot. It swished in—nothing but net—and he jogged to retrieve the ball.

I shrugged. "She's in a bind, I'm helping her out." I bounced the ball from one hand to the other. "If it means I get to make out with her again like Friday night, I'll be her fake date for as long as she wants. It was hot as hell."

Something strangely possessive had burned through me when I'd spotted Monty the other night. Some desperate frat bro had been leaning into her, obviously looking to score, and it had riled me in a way I couldn't understand. We'd kissed once, I had no claim to the girl. But before I knew what I was doing, I had stalked across the room and claimed her as mine.

Not that I was complaining about getting another chance to taste her.

Her ex being there had been a convenient excuse, right up until he'd interrupted us. Monty had come back to the kitchen after talking to him, grabbed her friend, and muttered a vague excuse before bailing.

Bant took another shot, swearing when he missed again. "So, you're just going to play house and never get laid again?"

Van halted, gripping the ball with both hands. "Wait, you can't hook up with anyone else?"

I'd been blinded by thoughts of Monty's lips when we'd kissed, the feel of her body pressed against mine and the small smiles she gave me when she flirted. Hell, the thought of her tongue in my mouth and her smoking hot body in my hands was getting me half hard right now. I'd been so focused on getting another shot with her, the thought of hooking up with anyone else hadn't crossed my mind. Which was definitely a first for me.

I had a reputation for a short attention span. It wasn't exactly intentional. I just had no desire for anything more than a surface-level connection. It wasn't that I intended to be alone forever, but I was focused on being drafted into the NBA. There'd be plenty of time for relationships and all the complications they brought after I'd made a name for myself in the pros.

"Ohhh shit," Bant said, a wide grin spreading across his face. "Look at that, our boy's got it bad."

"Fuck off." I pitched the basketball at his head.

He caught it before it clocked him in the face, sending it right back.

"Don't try to deny it," Bant said, laughing. "You've got major wood for this girl."

Sure, if Monty wanted to hook up, my pants would be undone before she'd even finished asking. But it wasn't like I was about to drop down and pop the question. I liked kissing her. Sue me.

Before I could tell Bant where to go, a shrill whistle cut through the gym.

"Wright, Bantempelli, any chance of some actual practice happening? Vandenberg is the only one who's knocked down a shot," Coach called. "Bantempelli couldn't hit the board if we got him a step ladder and sat him under the basket."

Van snorted, turning away so Coach wouldn't catch him laughing.

"And Wright's been fondling that ball all session. You going to shoot it or invite it to snuggle?"

I had the good sense to keep my mouth shut and act contrite or the whole team would be running suicides. My teammates would murder me if I brought that on us again.

"Sorry, Coach." I threw the ball towards the hoop, sinking the shot.

"Better." He turned back to the drills he was running with the freshmen.

"Shit, who pissed in his Cheerios today?" Bant asked.

Van sunk another three-pointer. "Maybe we should find Coach a fake girlfriend, since having one seems to be putting a semi in West's shorts."

"He's married, jackass." I took a jump shot, the swish of the net as satisfying as ever.

We worked hard for the next hour and a half, running drills before suiting up for a practice game. When practice was winding down, Coach pulled me aside.

"I'm sorry for slacking at the start of practice, Coach. It won't happen again."

And I meant it. If I was going to make it to the NBA, I had to play hard and train harder.

"I'll let it slide, but you better focus up, son. I've had some interesting emails this past week."

That had my attention.

"A couple of scouts from the NBA are going to be checking out our games this season, and most of them are going to be looking at you." He clapped a hand on my shoulder. "This is everything you've been working towards, which means it's time to take it to the next level and show them what you're made of. Understood?"

I nodded, my mind racing. This was my shot at getting drafted, which meant this season was the most important one I'd ever play. I couldn't let anything distract me from tearing up the court.

"Understood, Coach. I won't let you down."

"I know you won't, but it's not about me. It's about making sure you don't let yourself down. You've got a hell of a lot of talent, Wright, and the work ethic to match. You keep your head down and focus on the game, and I know you can go all the way."

My chest swelled with pride. The NBA was the only thing I'd ever wanted for myself.

And I'd do anything to make it happen.

Chapter Five

MONTY

"What's going on with you and the King of Campus?" Stella asked as we made our way through the dining hall in search of a table.

It was peak dinner time at Drysdale Hall, the biggest dining hall on campus, which meant the place was packed. With the hectic week of classes I'd had, the chaos was the last thing I felt like contending with. But it easily had the best food and I hadn't wanted to miss out on dinner with Stella and Imogen, given we'd all been so busy this week we'd barely seen each other.

"There's nothing going on. He helped me out of a situation with Alec, that's all," I said as I followed Stella, heading for a free table in the back.

I hadn't seen or heard from West since making out with him at that party.

Well, that wasn't entirely true. I'd spotted him a couple times on campus.

Chapter Six

MONTY

I was blinded by sunshine as I stepped out of my three-hour creative writing workshop. It had been a shame to waste such a perfect day sitting inside, but at least I'd made some serious headway on my final writing piece due at the end of the semester. My writing professor had given me really positive feedback on my plot direction and asked me to consider writing an entry for a prestigious short story competition that was opening soon. I'd need to write a new story from scratch, but that wasn't too hard to manage given I was already ahead of schedule with my end-of-semester piece. First prize in the contest was two thousand dollars, plus the prestige of winning, and my professor believed I had a real chance at placing. Even if I didn't win, the top ten entries got published in an anthology. I'd be a real published author before I'd even graduated.

I left the class feeling the most confident and upbeat I had since arriving at Pierson.

That was until I started down the walkway and Alec stepped in my path.

"Hey Monty, how was class?"

He gave me a broad smile, standing a little too close. My expression instantly shuttered. Was he really going to pretend like our conversation at the frat party never happened?

"Fine, thanks."

I started down the walkway again, praying he wouldn't follow me, but he fell into step beside me.

"How have you been? I've missed you," he said, throwing me glances as we navigated through the bustle of students. "We haven't spoken much lately."

I stopped, turning to face him. "Alec…"

"I saw you in the cafeteria yesterday. You didn't sit with your boyfriend."

His tone was edged with accusation, and my stomach tightened at the idea Alec had been watching me.

"We were having dinner with our own friends," I said, chastising myself for letting him bait me. I didn't owe him an explanation for my behavior.

I didn't owe him anything at all.

Turning on my heel, I dodged a trio of seniors. Alec got caught behind them, and I quickened my pace, trying to put some distance between us.

But he hurried after me, undeterred. "You haven't been replying to my messages."

His hand brushed mine as though he were trying to hold it, and I snatched it away from him, almost hitting a guy in the face who was walking in the opposite direction. I grimaced in apology but didn't slow down. If I didn't stop to talk, maybe Alec would get the message and leave me the hell alone.

"When I didn't hear back from you, I checked in with your mom, and she said you changed your number. She gave me your new one," Alec said.

I stopped still, staring at him. What about our last conversation had made him believe *that* is something I would have wanted?

I hadn't spoken to my mom via more than a text message in weeks, not since I'd first arrived at Pierson. It was the longest I'd gone without speaking to her or my dad since I'd left for college, but I'd been caught up settling into my dorm with Imogen and Stella and starting my new classes.

As well as dealing with Alec.

My parents had always liked him when we'd been together, and our moms played tennis together once a week back home. My mom and dad had been supportive but a little disappointed when I'd told them I'd ended it with Alec before leaving for college. But if I'd told them about the way he'd been acting since, my mom never would have given him my number.

A wave of homesickness swept over me. I missed home so much. And the piece of it standing in front of me no longer offered any sort of comfort. Only anxiety.

"Look, Alec, I don't know how else to say it. But I meant it when I asked you to leave me alone. Please don't text me and stop showing up outside my classes."

I stopped short of telling him he was starting to scare me. I didn't want to give him that power and I didn't want him to know his behavior was affecting me that way.

He reached out to tuck my hair behind my ear, and I flinched away from him in shock. Anger flared in his eyes.

Without a word, I took off down the path.

What the hell was wrong with him? I tell him to leave me alone and he takes that as an invitation to touch me?

I hurried into the courtyard at the end of the walkway, hoping to get lost in the bustle of students heading to class or the library or the dorms. A glimpse of the navy and white Pierson basketball uniforms caught my eye across the courtyard.

Please let West be with them.

I edged through the crowd. West was glancing at the passing students, laughing with Bant and another guy I didn't know. He spotted me, his brow creasing at whatever expression he read on my face. When I stopped beside him a little out of breath, he slung an arm around my shoulders and tucked me to his side.

"You okay, babe?"

He frowned, pressing a kiss to the top of my head in a move that was so achingly sweet I practically melted on the spot. Why had I been so worried about running into him after our make-out at the frat party?

I tilted my face up, trying to force a confident smile. I scanned the students for Alec, desperately hoping West's presence was enough to deter him from trying to approach me again.

The friend of West's I didn't know stared back at me in surprise. He had basketball player written all over him – black, tall and one hell of a toned body, with deep brown eyes and a smile like a naughty schoolboy.

"I'm sorry... you okay, *babe*?" he asked.

Bant shifted on his feet, glancing at West. "Yeah... so, Wright has a girlfriend now."

I stiffened. We'd never spoken about this whole fake dating ruse beyond fooling Alec in the quad or at the frat party. I didn't want West to have to lie to his friends and pretend we were together every time my ex-boyfriend showed up. I didn't even know the guy in front of me, but I hated that West was lying to him for me.

"Since when do you do girlfriends?" the guy said, giving me the once over.

It wasn't sleazy or judgey. More... curious.

West shrugged. "Since now."

"Come on, Davis," Bant said, clapping him on the shoulder and turning him in the direction of the dining hall. "We've got two hours before practice which means we could take down two meatball subs before we have to hit the court."

"Man, I could smash at least three," Davis said.

"Catch you guys later," Bant called to us, giving Davis a friendly shove in the direction of the dining hall.

West dropped his arm from my shoulders, turning to face me. "Did you run into Alec?"

"Is it that obvious?" I asked, blowing out a long breath.

"The look on your face when you came over here was pretty telling. Is he still bothering you?"

"It's fine," I lied. "He just seems to be popping up a little more often lately."

Those blue eyes stared back at me with an intensity that made me fidget. "Do you think you should maybe report him to campus police?"

I shook my head. "I don't want to make a fuss. He's just having some trouble letting go. He'll move on soon."

West didn't look convinced, but he didn't push it.

A rush of students filtered around us, making me suddenly aware that we were standing in the middle of the courtyard.

He took my hand, leading us out of the way. "Listen, I've got an idea but it's kind of wild."

My emotions were already running wild after my run-in with Alec, a little more would hardly make a difference.

"Hit me. I love wild. I'm all about wild," I said.

West's eyebrows crept up his forehead in a look that said he was clearly picturing us getting wild in the bedroom.

I swatted at his chest, and he chuckled. "I can't control where my mind goes when you say things like that."

"Well, try. You don't have to be a horny fuckboy every second of the day."

He pretended to be wounded. "I have so much more to offer the women of this world than endless sexual opportunities, Monty."

I rolled my eyes, noting the steady stream of girls glancing at West with interest as they passed us. "Are you going to tell me this wild idea or not?"

He nodded. "I think it's a solution to both our problems."

"I wasn't aware you had problems."

He raised an amused eyebrow. "Oh, I see. She thinks she has the monopoly on annoying exes?"

"You have an annoying ex?" I asked, doubt coloring my tone. "Wouldn't that involve actually committing to someone for more than one night?"

His eyes narrowed on me. "You've got me there, but I can still help you out."

"By all means, let's hear it."

"Alec doesn't really seem to be getting the message to chill the fuck out," he said, blue eyes earnest. "So maybe I should help you out on a more permanent basis."

"Help me out how?"

"By fake dating." He smiled. "For real."

I blinked. Was he asking me out? Or pretending to ask me out? Or asking me out but only to play pretend?

"Us dating would keep Alec away," West went on. "And get some of the crazy basketball groupies off my back. It's win-win for both of us."

I frowned. "And you'd be okay with lying to people?"

He nodded in greeting at a girl who called his name as she passed.

"I just lied to Davis and the world didn't end. And the important people like Bant and Van and Imogen already know the truth."

His gaze landed on me, eyes filled with expectation.

Faking a relationship with West definitely had its appeal. But getting mixed up in any kind of relationship when I was still dealing with the remnants of my last one would only lead to more drama. And that was the last thing I wanted right now.

Besides, if I was going to be in a relationship, I wanted it to be real. Given West's total aversion to commitment, there was no way he was the guy for that. Sure, we could make out and have fun doing it, but I wasn't going to sleep with him. And I didn't need to ask to know that he wasn't about to stop sleeping around in order to help me either.

"I appreciate the offer and believe me when I say it's a hard one to turn down."

His expression shifted. "But you're going to?"

I nodded. "You have no idea how much I appreciate you helping me out, you've saved me so many times already, and you were so chill about me jumping you in the quad. But I have to deal with Alec at some point, right?"

He ran a hand through his hair, trying to mask his surprise. "Yeah, of course."

All West and I had done was kiss a few times. Any connection we might have formed hadn't even gotten off the ground yet. So why did this suddenly feel like an incredibly awkward breakup?

I gripped the straps of my backpack and started to back away.

"Thanks for everything, West, really." I gave him a small smile. "I guess I'll see you around?"

Chapter Seven

"Don't take this the wrong way man, but you're playing like shit," Bant said, working to catch his breath after we were subbed off the court for a break.

I slumped on the bench, propping my elbows on my knees and hanging my head in my hands in frustration.

I was so off my game tonight, it was embarrassing.

The crowd was so damn loud, cheering every run down the court and going off every time we scored. We were only nine points down and there was still plenty of time to win it, but so far it wasn't due to any kind of stellar performance from me. Even the freshmen were balling better than I was right now. I prayed there were no scouts here to witness my undoing.

My usual Friday routine before a Saturday game was to cut out early after practice to meet a girl back at the house. We'd hang out, maybe order a pizza or watch a movie, before heading up to my room to bang it out. She'd be gone by eight, and I'd sleep like the dead afterwards. It was part of what had earned me my Campus King status, but the girls were always willing participants. Some of them were even regulars at their own insistence.

Only yesterday, instead of getting laid, I'd spent it getting shut down by Monty.

I don't even know how it happened. One minute I'd been joking around with Bant and Davis before practice and the next I was offering to fake date her. When I'd seen the worry—no, the fear—in her eyes that she was working so hard to hide as she powered across the courtyard to get away from her stalker ex, an unexpected need to protect her had flared inside me. Before reality could catch up with my damn mouth, I'd offered to fake it with her on a more permanent basis.

I'd thought after the frat party we had some kind of a connection. It didn't occur to me that she might outright reject me. Offering to fake date Monty was more than I'd offered any girl in a long time. Yet she couldn't get away fast enough.

'I guess I'll see you around?'

The questioning tone was the killer; like she wasn't sure if she would or not.

Which meant Monty was gone, and I was stuck whining about it in my head like a little bitch, my mixed-up feelings playing out on the court. All because one girl in a sea of thousands had knocked me back.

I needed a head check.

"Wright!" Coach called. "You got your head together enough to get on the court and win us this game?"

I pushed to my feet, stretching my neck from side to side and shaking out all thoughts of girls and feelings and shit I had no control over.

This game I could control.

I was the goddamn star of the Pierson basketball team, and I was going to play like it.

"Yeah, Coach," I said, adrenaline pumping through me as I soaked up the roar of the Pierson fans. "I can win it."

* * *

Turns out that was a fucking lie.

Not only did I not win us the game, I lost my head and fouled out before the fourth quarter.

Coach was livid. My teammates were salty as fuck with me but had the good sense to keep it to themselves. Only Williams, a senior and the team captain, had the balls to come near me and my dark mood in the locker room after the game.

"Don't worry about it, man," he said, clapping me on the shoulder. "Can't win them all."

I'd offered him a weak smile in return. If there was a scout in the stadium tonight I was done. Nothing about my game had been NBA material.

But I was still West-fucking-Wright. And that meant when I wanted to get wasted to forget my problems and my shitty game, there were plenty of people willing to follow me down to the bottom of a bottle. Or six.

Which was why the living room of the basketball house near Greek Row that I shared with Van, Davis, Bant and five other guys from the team was currently packed with people getting drunk and generally having a good time.

Davis was in the kitchen making out with some senior girl who was sitting on the kitchen counter in her bra sucking his face off, the two of them ignoring repeated suggestions to take it upstairs. But that was Davis for you. Single-minded focus and zero fucks to give.

Three girls in the shortest skirts and highest heels I'd ever seen danced on the coffee table in front of me in the living room, hips swaying to the thumping bass coming from the speakers. I watched them absently from my armchair, a bottle of some designer Japanese beer Bant had scored in an effort to cheer me up hanging from my fingers. Now on beer number six, I was comfortably wasted and had no plans to move for the rest of the night. Unless it was to get another drink.

"You want to talk about it?" Van asked from the couch.

I slid my gaze to him. "Not at all."

He smirked. "Getting plastered it is, then."

He raised his beer in my direction, and I returned the gesture, bringing the bottle to my lips and taking a long pull. The girl closest to me on the table shot me a flirtatious smile, swaying her hips wider and giving me an eyeful of the hot-pink thong under her skirt.

If I weren't intent on wallowing in my own self-pity, I probably would have taken her up to my room already.

Fuck basketball.

Fuck winning.

And fuck feelings.

Why the hell had I let Monty's rejection get so far under my skin when we hadn't even slept together? This was exactly why I didn't get attached. It wasn't just that it would fuck with my fast-track to the NBA; I'd learned a long time ago that catching any sort of feelings was a one-way ticket to pain and disappointment. I had my parents to blame for that. They were the reason I avoided any kind of deeper emotional connection.

Their marriage was a sham. My father had been

sleeping with his twenty-seven-year-old assistant for the past four years, taking her on "business trips" just so he could bang her for three days straight before coming home to my mom and playing happy families in front of their friends. Mom was no better. A few years ago, I'd walked in on her going at it with the thirty-something-year-old pool guy.

Talk about cliché.

The image was seared into my mind, no matter how hard I tried to shake it. I'd contemplated washing my eyes out with acid, but being able to see the ball coming at me on the court was a pretty crucial skill.

It seemed I was more like my mom than I'd thought though, because unlike my dad, it was increasingly hard to keep up with my mom's latest bed buddy. My parents weren't exactly the poster people for functioning monogamy, and I had no desire to follow them down the same path. To me, relationships were a recipe for betrayal.

Hard pass. I was more than happy to stick to casual. At least that was honest.

Shoving a hand through my hair, I tried to shake off my dark mood. There was one quick way to get Monty's rejection and my crappy performance on the court out of my head.

Sitting forward, I pressed my elbows to my knees, staring up at the girl dancing on the table. She smiled down at me, hips swaying seductively.

I was about to call her over to sit on my lap and erase all thoughts of the hot, leggy brunette who'd made it perfectly clear yesterday that she didn't need me, when a trio of heels came through the front door with a gust of cold night air.

"Quad Girl!" Van called from the sofa, and Monty

appeared in the doorway to the living room, because clearly the universe wasn't done fucking with me tonight.

She was with Imogen and her other friend...Stella, I think?

She looked hot as fuck in a pair of black, skin-tight leather pants, red fuck-me heels and a grey band t-shirt tied at her waist. Her long brown hair fell over her shoulders in waves as she shucked off her coat and hung it by the front door, and my mind instantly jumped to all the ways I wanted to have her hair draped over me.

She stared at me, her face colored with surprise. "What are you doing here?"

I huffed a humorless laugh. "Nice to see you too, Quad Girl."

She stalked toward me, and I couldn't tear my eyes away from her legs in those pants, picturing what they'd feel like wrapped around me. The thought made my cock stir in my shorts.

"Are you drunk?" she asked, peering down at me.

I kept my face purposefully blank. "Not even close. And I live here," I said in answer to her previous question.

Her eyes widened. "You live here?"

"Yep," I said, popping the P. "Want to see my bedroom?"

She rolled her eyes. "You are drunk. Your flirting usually has way more finesse than that."

Her friends motioned to her that they were heading to the kitchen, and she nodded, taking a seat on the sofa next to my armchair. She was a little too close to Van and a little too far away from me for my liking.

"Bad game?"

I slid my gaze to her. "No, I played great."

"That's not what I heard."

Fan-fucking-tastic. Word of my poor form was getting around.

At least she hadn't been there to witness my failure firsthand.

I narrowed my eyes at her. "Way to really kick a guy when he's down, Monty."

She smiled, and I wanted to spend the rest of the night watching her do it.

For fuck's sake. Why was I so hung up on this girl after a couple of make-outs?

"It was one bad game, West. You'll kill it next time. You're still the team stud with the prettiest face and the hottest body, so at least you've got that going for you."

I raised an eyebrow at her and smacked my hand against my thigh, indicating to my lap. "Hop on, I'll let you take the hottest body on the team for a test drive."

This time she outright laughed, and I couldn't help the smile that spread across my face.

"Wow, Monty, I didn't know you could work miracles," Van said, his girlfriend, Annabelle, now draped in his lap. "It usually takes hours and a whole case of beer before West will crack a smile after a bad game."

"I must be the West whisperer," she said, those grey-blue eyes connecting with mine.

She had no idea how true that was.

Chapter Eight

MONTY

Are you going to call me back?

It's Alec. But I know you know that.

Call me back. I miss you x

I saw you in the quad today. You look beautiful with your hair like that.

Monty, I'm not going to let this go. We belong together.

Still not answering my calls?

I know you're getting my texts. Answer me, Monty.

Saw your new "boyfriend" today. You weren't with him and I know it's because you still want to be with me.

It's Friday night and I can't stop thinking about you. What are you doing? Please answer my calls.

Monty, I don't know what else I can do to show you how much I care about you.

I transferred to Pierson to be with you. If that doesn't show you how much I love you, I don't know what will.

Came by your dorm today, but Stella said you were out. She told me not to come back, but that's not what you want, is it Monty?

I t had been weeks.

Weeks of non-stop messaging from Alec. Some days it was eight messages at a time, others it was one. But he never let me forget that he was always right there.

It was his last two messages that freaked me out the most. Or maybe it was the entire, continuous thread, sitting there plain as day that made my skin crawl. There was no way this could be played off as a guy who was struggling to fit in and looking for the familiarity of home. It was much more than that.

The more silent I was, the more incessant Alec's texts

became. Stella and Imogen had tried to convince me repeatedly to go to the police, but I couldn't do it. It was my fault for letting it get this far, and I was way too embarrassed to go and share the details of Alec's obsessive behavior with the authorities, especially when his uncle was one of them. There was a chance they might not even believe me, brushing it off as some petty breakup drama leftover from high school.

Alec just needed more time to settle into Pierson. Once he made friends and focused on his classes, he'd lose interest in me.

But that didn't mean his messages didn't unsettle me. Especially the last one about showing up at my dorm.

How would he even know where I lived unless he'd followed me home?

The thought sent a cold shiver hurtling down my spine.

With Stella's commitments as an art major keeping her in the studio more often than not, especially after hours, and Imogen working on a group project for her psychology class, I'd been alone in our dorm most nights this week. Tonight was one of those nights.

I checked the lock on the suite door for the fourth time, then I inwardly chastised myself.

Alec wasn't going to break into my dorm. The worst he'd do would be to turn up and demand a conversation... *right?*

Leaning against the counter of our small kitchenette, I clutched a mug of tea in one hand, chewing on my thumbnail on the other.

West's offer to fake date was looking pretty damn good right now.

I'd been stupid to knock it back on the spot without taking the time to consider exactly what dealing with Alec on my own would involve. So far, it meant ignoring endless and persistent texts and stressing that he was going to turn up at my door, or my classes or the library at any moment. It was bad enough that he accosted me outside my classes, now I couldn't escape him at my dorm either.

At the very least if I'd accepted West's offer I'd still have him as friend to call right now when I was alone and freaked out. He'd never once judged me for my reactions to Alec, just offered a friendly shoulder to lean on. And I could really use that right now. But I hadn't seen West since the party at the basketball house that I hadn't known was the basketball house when I'd agreed to go along. He had clearly been looking to drown his sorrows that night after his bad game, but we'd still managed to have fun.

Part of me missed him, which was ridiculous. I barely knew the guy.

Then again, maybe it was West's reassuring presence I missed most. So far he'd been the only thing that had deterred Alec in any real way. My repeated pleas with him to leave me alone were clearly having no effect.

But West wasn't a toy I could pick up and put down as I pleased. He'd made me an offer and I'd turned him down, now we'd both moved on with our lives. It was hardly a surprise given the guy had a steady stream of girls waiting to jump into his bed the moment I'd said no to him.

Alec was my problem. One I needed to work out how to fix fast.

Sighing, I tossed the rest of my tea down the sink and headed for my room.

There was nothing a good night's sleep couldn't fix, right? Everything would look better in the morning.

* * *

I woke to four missed calls and another two text messages from Alec.

> *You still love me, Monty. I'm not giving up until I get you back because we're meant to be together. You'll see that eventually.*
>
> *I'm at your door, open up. I know you're alone.*

My stomach dropped as I read the last one, dread pooling in my gut.

How the hell had he known I'd been home alone?

I walked to class, stewing over the messages and shooting furtive glances over my shoulder looking for Alec. Surely he wasn't following me every minute of the day, I told myself. He had to have his own classes to go to.

But straying that close to truly paranoid didn't stop me from checking over my shoulder every time I left a lecture hall or workshop room after missing out on what was no doubt crucial information in just about every class because I couldn't stay focused. I was surrounded by people, but I still felt totally exposed.

By the time the sun set at the end of the day, I was emotionally frayed, fed up and a little angry. I didn't want to spend another day or even another minute looking over my shoulder or triple-checking the locks on the common room door, all because Alec couldn't let go of a relationship that had ended more than a year ago. I wanted this to end, and Alec had made it clear that telling him to move on wasn't enough. I'd reached my limit.

Which is how I found myself at the basketball stadium at the end of practice.

I scanned the courts looking for that familiar dark hair and tall athletic body. Only they were all tall, athletic bodies here.

"Who you looking for?" a seriously tall black guy asked, his southern accent strong.

"West Wright?"

The skinny kid behind him, clearly a freshman, snorted. "Aren't they all."

The tall guy shot him a look and pitched a basketball at him. The freshman wasn't fast enough to react, and it clocked him in the stomach. "Don't speak to a lady like that."

The freshman doubled over, groaning.

Tall Guy ignored him, turning back to me. "You just missed him."

Damn it.

I glanced at the windows along the ceiling, the sky darkening outside. I had to make this quick and get back to my dorm. I didn't make a habit of walking the campus at night, but with how freaked out I'd been feeling, I didn't want to risk it at all.

I thanked Tall Guy and wandered back the way I'd come, walking the halls in search of the locker room.

I didn't plan to go in, but maybe I could catch West on his way out. Now that I'd committed to this idea, I was determined to see it through. I totally expected him to turn me down, given I'd already rejected him once, but I was scared and desperate enough to try.

Lost in my own head, I didn't notice the cheerleader and basketball player leaning against the wall until I'd almost reached them. Still dressed in full uniform, the player's back was to me, his forearm resting on the wall above the girl's head. She stared up at him with a look of adoration, and he leaned in to whisper in her ear, her laughter echoing down the hall.

I moved closer, trying to make out the name across the back of the jersey.

Wright. My stomach dropped.

"West?"

He looked at me over his shoulder, pushing off the wall. "Monty? What are you doing here?"

I bit the inside of my cheek. This was a terrible idea. He'd clearly moved on and forgotten all about me.

"Uh, I was looking for you," I said, sliding my hands in the back pockets of my jeans to stop me from fidgeting.

West's face lit with surprise. "You were?"

I nodded, glancing at the cheerleader behind him.

"West?" She peered up at him. "Are we still going back to my place?"

He looked back at her. "Another time?"

Annoyance washed over her, and she looked me up and down before storming down the hall with a small huff.

West closed the space between us. "Is everything okay?"

I stalled. How did you ask a guy to be your fake boyfriend when he'd already offered it once and you'd turned him down?

"Hey," he said, reading the worry on my face and taking my hand. "What's up?"

I took a deep breath. *Just bite the bullet and ask.*

"Alec has been... escalating," I said, staring back at him. "I'm starting to get freaked out, and I'm hoping your previous offer to be my fake muscle still stands."

If he'd been surprised to see me here, he was even more surprised now.

"You want to fake date me?"

I nodded, and he studied me for a long moment, blue eyes scanning my face.

Then he shrugged, his face splitting into a grin.

"Sure, babe. Count me in."

* * *

"We need to set some ground rules," I said from the passenger seat of West's black Mercedes G wagon.

After I'd shown him Alec's text messages, he'd taken me back to my dorm and told me to pack a bag because I was staying with him tonight. There had been no objection from me. Alec's behavior had unsettled me more than I was willing to admit and spending the night at West's place when it was filled with giant basketball players was exactly the kind of safety I was looking for.

"Okay," West said, glancing at me while still trying to watch the road. "You throw some rules out, and I'll veto the ones I don't like."

"They're not negotiable."

He grinned. "Everything in life is negotiable."

"That's not even remotely true, what about..." I held up a hand, stopping myself from going down the life-philoso-phies-of-West-Wright rabbit hole. "You know what, I'm not even going to go there right now. We're talking about ground rules."

He rested his wrist over the top of the steering wheel, giving me a cocky smile. "Okay, shoot."

"Fine. Rule number one... no sex."

"Veto!"

I rolled my eyes. "You're not going to get me to sleep with you."

West's face creased with mock outrage. "Get you to? Babe, you're going to want to do it. You'll be begging me, in fact."

His unflinching self-assurance made me laugh. "Oh okay, superstar. You think you're so irresistible that I won't be able to control myself?"

His eyes lit with amusement, and I tried not to swoon at the sight. "Something like that."

God, what must it be like to live with West-level confidence?

"Whatever you say, Romeo."

He stopped at a red light, fingers tapping the gear shift to a song by The Weeknd playing low on the radio.

"Rule number two. No revealing it's a fake relationship to anyone who doesn't already know." This wouldn't work if all my friends and half the basketball team knew we were faking it. "What? No objection to that one?"

West shot me a sideways smile, accelerating when the light turned green. "Do you want me to object to it?"

"No, just checking."

I took a deep breath, psyching myself up to deliver the clincher.

"Rule number three, and this one is going to be hard for you," I said, watching him for his reaction. "No sleeping with other people."

He glanced at me again, eyes smiling. "Waiting for me to veto that one too?"

"Yeah, kind of."

He shrugged. "I'm not going to."

I sat up straighter in my chair, turning towards him. "Wait a second, you're telling me you're going to agree that we won't have sex with each other, but also promise that you won't have sex with other people?"

He pulled up outside the house, switching off the engine and turning to face me. "First of all, our fake relationship isn't going to be very convincing if we're both sleeping with other people every other week."

I liked the fact that he said 'we' instead of 'he', as though I had guys on speed dial ready to come over and fuck me whenever I felt like it. One, I hated hook-ups. And two, it wouldn't be true even if I was into them.

"And second of all?" I asked.

His smile filled with mischief. "We don't have to worry because I meant it when I said you'd be begging me to sleep with you."

Chapter Nine

As soon as we walked through the door, I took Monty's bag up to my room. Then we parked on the couch, ordered a pizza and proceeded to drown our problems in alcohol.

Alec was a topic Monty was clearly trying to avoid dealing with, but given how scared she'd looked when she'd turned up at the stadium tonight, I didn't want to push it. If hiding out with me made her feel safe, I was happy to be her bodyguard for as long as she needed.

She wasn't interested in me as anything more than a buffer between her and her ex, that much was clear. And while rejection was a new thing for me, it was probably for the best. Basketball had to be my focus. I wasn't sure I was even capable of the kind of monogamy required for a real connection. But that didn't mean I'd turn down the chance to spend more time with her. Or sleep with her. The few times we'd made out had been off-the-charts hot, which meant sex between us was guaranteed to be one hell of a ride. Shame she'd slapped a 'no sex' rule on this fake relationship faster than I could wink in her direction. On the other hand, I've never shied away from a challenge.

"I have two thoughts," she said from across the low coffee table, taking another sip of the spicy margaritas I'd made — my specialty.

"Oh, only two?"

"The first..." she said, ignoring me. "...is that you make an excellent cocktail."

She gave the glass in her hand a little shake, margarita sloshing over the side.

"And the second?"

"The second is that you suck at this game!"

She motioned to the game of Guess Who spread out in front of us.

I scowled. "Because you're a nut job who won't let us play by the rules!"

"Where's the fun in that?" She waved a hand in dismissal. "Does your character have brown eyes? Does your character have white hair? Is your character black? Snore!"

I tried to hide my amusement at how drunk she was. She was already on her third margarita, while I was still on my first. Coach had a rule about us drinking more than a beer or two per week during the season and given we were five games in and four-and-one on the board, he definitely wouldn't be up for me downing cocktails mid-week. But getting drunk and forgetting everything had been the goal for Monty tonight, and so far, she was taking to it with the dedication of a frat boy trying to nail a cheerleader.

"Go on, ask me a question then," I said, bringing her back to the game.

"Does your character look like someone who went to horse camp in eighth grade?"

I levelled her with a flat stare. "No...?"

She flicked down several of her game pieces, smiling brightly at me. "Your turn."

"Does your character look like they're into toe kink?" I tried.

Her eyes lit up. "Yes!"

She looked so fucking cute nodding emphatically at the suggestion the mostly middle-aged Guess Who characters could be into sucking toes that I wanted to tug her close and kiss her until she moaned for more.

Instead, I flicked some random game pieces down to appease her, knocking back my margarita and reaching for the pitcher to refill both our glasses. It had been too long since I'd just hung out with a girl who wasn't trying to get into my bed or who wasn't already dating one of my teammates. I'd forgotten how much fun it could be to just chill.

"Does your character look like someone who'd own nipple clamps?" she asked, and I snorted a laugh.

"What the hell kind of question is that?"

She screwed up her nose. "Too specific? What about someone who looks like they have a secret sex toy collection?"

I stared at the character card, trying to work out if Alan could be secretly hiding a box of dildos under his bed.

"Probably."

She clapped happily, knocking down several more pieces before downing the drink I'd just poured her.

"How are you so good at making these?" she said, pouting at the bottom of her empty glass and discarding it on the table. At least she only had to stumble upstairs to my room to pass out later.

"I worked as a waiter at Dave and Buster's every Sunday in high school. My parents thought it would keep me out of trouble when I wasn't playing basketball and teach me some responsibility. I wasn't supposed to work behind the bar when I was underage, but the owner liked me so she taught me how to make a drink or two."

Monty sat back in her chair, crossing her arms over her chest. "Well, thank you, rule breaking boss in high school. It's really paid off for college Monty."

I smiled, shaking my head. The margaritas had certainly loosened her up. The tension in her shoulders was gone, along with the worry behind her eyes.

"I have a question for you," I said, leaning forward to rest my elbows on my knees.

She stared back at me with wide grey-blue eyes, waiting.

"Are you going to come to my game this weekend?"

A frown creased her brow. "Do you want me to?"

I shrugged. "Some of the girlfriends do, like Van's girl, Annabelle. And some of the others."

She leaned forward mirroring me, her expression suddenly serious. "Do I have to wear your basketball jacket and make out with you behind the bleachers?"

"Jacket, no. Making out under the stands..." I rubbed my jaw. "You have my attention."

She sat back, and I grabbed my glass off the table, taking a sip and hating that there was so much space between us again. The more we drank the closer I wanted her.

"At least you didn't ask me to blow you under the bleachers," she said casually.

I choked on my drink, practically coughing up a lung. "I didn't realize that option was on the table," I said, wiping my chin.

She lifted one shoulder in a shrug, a small smile playing on her perfect mouth.

She was messing with me, but I didn't care one bit. Just the thought of her lips on my dick was enough to have me sporting a semi.

She glanced up, eyes laced with an intensity I hadn't seen from her before.

Was she actually considering blowing me right now?

I hoped I was right and it was only a matter of time before she was begging me to break the no-sex rule between us, but I thought she'd hold out longer than a couple of hours.

"West?"

My dick twitched in anticipation.

"Yeah?"

She smiled. "Are you Alan?"

Chapter Ten

MONTY

I woke in a strange bed, an arm flung over my waist, my head pounding and mouth full of sand. Or at least it felt that way.

West. I was in West's bed.

I scrambled to lift the sheets to find I was still dressed in last night's clothes.

We didn't have sex.

I couldn't tell if it was relief or disappointment that flashed through me at the realization.

West stirred behind me, pressing a kiss to my shoulder. "Morning, gorgeous."

"Morning."

He pulled me tighter against him, and I stiffened. It wasn't that I didn't want to snuggle him. The way my body lit up from even the slightest touch from him was proof of how much I wanted him. But we had to draw the line somewhere. We were fake dating. We couldn't let things get blurred if we wanted to come out the other side of this. The thought of dealing with Alec and West, along with my ever-increasing course load, was almost enough to tip me over the edge into insanity.

West sighed. "You don't need to do that."

"Do what?"

"Get all in your head about waking up in my bed or what we agreed to last night."

I glanced at him over my shoulder. "How did you know I was thinking about that?"

"Because trying to hold you right now is like spooning an ironing board."

"Wow, what a sexy comparison," I said, rolling in his arms to face him.

He smiled, his eyes still closed, and I resisted the urge to kiss him.

Rein it in, Monty. He's not yours.

"Do it," West said, sliding a hand over my waist and tugging me closer. "You're thinking about how much you want to kiss me right now, then running through all the reasons why you shouldn't."

A smile spread across my face. How had he become such a Monty-whisperer in such a short amount of time?

His hand slid up my back, sending a delicious shiver across every inch of my skin, and I wriggled closer until my body was flush with his, the hard length of him jutting against my hip.

"Someone is happy to see me this morning," I said, a smile in my tone.

"I'm always happy to see you, babe."

The way the words fell from his mouth, it was easy to think he might actually mean them. But he probably said sweet things to every girl who woke in his bed.

The thought was like a bucket of ice water over my head, and I pulled away to sit up.

West stretched out beside me, the sheets slipping low, given me the perfect view of his bare torso. His body was absolute fire. Toned pecs, ridged abs and a deep V disappearing into his sweats that had me tucking my hands under my thighs to stop me from running my fingers—or my tongue—over every sexy inch of him.

Clearing my throat, I tore my eyes away. "I really need to take a shower."

"You take my bathroom, there are clean towels on the rail. I'll use the main bathroom, and meet you in the kitchen for breakfast in fifteen?"

I nodded, slipping from the bed to grab my bag.

"Just make sure you lock both doors. I share that bathroom with Bant. If he's home, you don't want him copping an eyeful so early in the morning and getting ideas."

I smiled at the protective sentiment and headed for the bathroom, throwing both the locks. It was surprisingly clean given it was regularly used by college ball players. I'd expected them to be slobs.

I strolled into the kitchen twenty minutes later to find West at the stove, dressed in a fresh pair of navy Pierson sweatpants and nothing else.

He was certainly trying hard to get me to cave on the no-sex rule by dressing like an athletic thirst trap.

"Hey," he said over his shoulder, the muscles of his back bunching and contracting as he cracked eggs into the frypan. "You like scrambled eggs?"

I slid into a seat at the counter with a groan. "Yes, please."

"How's your head?" West asked with a knowing smile.

"Pounding like a fifteen-year-old who got a drum set for Christmas."

He chuckled. "There's Tylenol in the cabinet there, and Gatorade in the fridge."

Sliding from my chair I collected both. "Pays to have a hangover in a house full of ball players. Where are your roommates, anyway?"

"Who knows? I gave up trying to keep track of those idiots a long time ago. Pretty sure Van's home, my captain Williams too. I think they got in late last night."

"So how many of you actually live here?"

The house was enormous. It didn't look like much from the front, but there were four bedrooms on the bottom level and at least five on the second.

"Nine. Jericho, Chen and Van live down here. Bant, Hernandez, Williams, Reggie and I are on the second level. Davis is in the attic bedroom. Don't know why when all he does is bitch about how long it takes him to get up to his room after a killer practice."

I mulled it over. "So, this is like a frat house but for basketball players?"

"Pretty much. It's just always been the basketball house, been that way for years. Usually it's for the junior and senior players and when they graduate the next crop move in. But Van, Bant and I managed to score three rooms last year when Van and I were sophomores. Bant was only a freshman."

"How did you pull that off? Because you're such a stud on the court?"

He smirked at me over his shoulder. "Not just on the court, babe."

I rolled my eyes. "You know, I don't even know what

you're studying. Seems like something a girlfriend should know."

"Applied Exercise Science," he said, focused on cooking.

Being interested in the way bodies moved and how to train them for greatness made sense given he was an athlete. It suited him.

His phone pinged on the counter beside me, and I glanced at it.

"Can you check that? It's probably Bant asking me to come pick him up from wherever he crashed last night."

Sliding from my stool, I picked up his phone, glancing at the message from someone named Tahlia.

Hey baby. Want me to come round before class and help you with your morning wood?

I put the phone down, sliding it back across the counter.

"Who is it?" West asked without turning around.

"Uh... not Bant."

He frowned, leaving the spatula on the counter to retrieve his phone. His eyebrows crept up his forehead as he read.

"You can reply if you want. Don't ignore her on my account," I said, hoping my tone was casual enough to hide my surprise.

I really had no claim to West. We'd only agreed to this whole fake dating thing last night, there hadn't been time yet for it to filter through the basketball crowd. But it didn't stop a spark of jealousy flaring inside me.

Boundaries. What we needed were boundaries. For both our sakes.

Instead, West closed the space between us, taking my hand and tugging me close, my hands landing on his perfectly sculpted pecs. This was the opposite of boundaries.

He stared down at me. "I committed to this with you last night. I'm not going to back out because a girl messaged me to hook-up. Besides, these are the kinds of situations my fake relationship with you is meant to be saving me from. Do you really think Tahlia is interested in me? Or just interested in saying she hooked up with me?"

I met his gaze, my brow pinching. "You really think that?"

"I know that. But it's getting old."

I'd been quick to judge West off his reputation as a player both on and off the court. But the way he'd protected me—more than once—from Alec's overzealous advances when he barely even knew me proved he was so much more than a campus fuckboy. If he weren't so painfully allergic to commitment, he'd be the perfect guy.

But his reputation made it clear long-term connections weren't his jam, and heartbreak wasn't mine. Not when I still had Alec's fallout to deal with.

"Monty..." West's eyes filled with heat, and he leaned towards me, closing the space between us.

I held my fingers to his lips, stilling him.

"I think we need to draw some lines between us. Just so we're clear on what's real and what's not."

"Okay..." His brow creased. "What does that mean?"

"We should probably stop making out all the time, but especially behind closed doors."

He tipped his head back and groaned. "Trust me when I say, we already make out way less than I want to."

Slipping from his grasp, I couldn't help my smile. He sure was good for my ego.

"It's making things messy. I mean, we're obviously attracted to each other. But if we're going to manage to stay friends at the end of this fake relationship, we probably need to set some boundaries."

"If you're worried that I'll fall in love with you if we make out, don't be."

And consider that ego he'd just inflated officially shot down.

I pulled a face. "Gee, thanks a lot."

He chuckled. "Not because you're not loveable, babe. But I'm just not into relationships. I don't know how to do them. Even with someone with a perfect peach of an ass like yours."

He grinned at me, and I tried to fight my smile in return, sliding back onto my stool. He'd just confirmed everything I'd already known, which meant even fantasizing about a connection with West was a waste of time. And a recipe for heartache.

"I think it's best if we draw a line and agree not to cross it."

He sighed, turning back to the cooktop. "When it comes to this kind of thing, I'm more of a do-what-I-want-and-worry-about-it-later type of guy."

No surprises there. A guy who hooked up as much as he did without catching feelings had to be sporting some kind of emotional armor. Worrying about it another day was West's.

He shrugged. "But sure, babe, whatever you want."

In theory, it was definitely what I wanted. Putting it

into practice was a little harder. But I needed to protect my heart. I couldn't get involved with anyone until I'd dealt with Alec and every negative encounter he brought with him.

West slid the eggs from the skillet onto two plates, placing one in front me, then pulling up a chair.

I picked up my fork. "Can I ask you something?"

He shoveled in a mouthful of eggs. "Shoot."

"Why did you offer to help me in the first place? Don't get me wrong, I'm grateful you did. But I guess I just don't understand why you'd agree to this when you're giving up so much. Given your reputation, you clearly haven't had an issue with sleeping with crazy female fans in the past. Why stop now?"

The question hung between us in the silence, something flickering behind his eyes. Then he shrugged, an easy grin spreading across his handsome face.

"Must be my knight in shining armor complex."

His response did nothing to assuage the feeling that I was burdening him with my problems.

I gave him a small smile. "That must be it."

Chapter Eleven

WEST

I was nursing a beer in a dark bar when movement near the door caught my eye. Imogen and Stella came through the crowd, Monty notably absent. When I'd texted her this afternoon she'd been in class and said she was going to meet her study group tonight.

It had been more than a week since we'd seen each other. I'd been busy with practice and game days, and she'd spent most of her time holed up in the library writing her contest submission. But there was no mistaking the flash of disappointment that reared in me when I saw she wasn't with her friends.

Fuck me. She wasn't even my real girlfriend, but I was sitting in a bar with my friends, pining for her like a jackass.

O'Reilly's bar was unexpectedly packed for a Thursday night. It was never quiet, not when it was one of only two bars close to campus, but tonight it was standing room only.

We'd somehow managed to snag a piece of prime real

estate—a booth in the back, large enough to accommodate all of us: Davis, Bant, Van, Annabelle, our teammate and housemate Hernandez, his girlfriend Harley and me. I sat at the edge of the round booth next to Annabelle, who was unusually quiet tonight.

I nudged her shoulder with mine. "You okay, Belle?"

"Yeah, I guess so," she said, toying with her glass.

I frowned. "That didn't sound convincing. Something going on?"

She glanced at Van across the booth. "Things have been a little off between Adam and I lately. He hasn't said anything to you, has he?"

He hadn't, but even if he did confide in me about his relationship with Annabelle, I wouldn't break bro-code and share it with her. I liked Annabelle, but my friendship with Van would always come first. We were teammates and brothers for life.

"He hasn't said anything to me." I took a sip of my beer, glancing at my best friend.

He was staring at something across the bar, the crowd blocking whatever it was. Then he glanced at Annabelle and sat straighter, reaching for his beer and joining the conversation with Bant and the others.

"Maybe I'm just being paranoid..." Annabelle said with a sigh.

"But?"

She leaned in, lowering her voice. "I think he might be cheating on me."

I stared down at her, hoping she was joking. But the worried pinch in her brow told me she was dead serious.

Van? Cheating? No way.

"He isn't that kind of guy, Belle."

She bit her lip, the action reminding me so much of Monty I wanted to slide my phone from my pocket and text her to find out where she was.

Why the hell was I getting so attached?

It's not like Monty had any problem keeping her distance. She'd totally shut down after reading that text from Tahlia and now she was all about boundaries—no sex was one thing, but no kissing?

What more did I need to convince myself she wasn't interested?

I shook her from my head and forced myself to focus on Annabelle.

"A few months ago, I would have said that Adam wasn't the cheating type too. But I think he hooked up with someone when we had that break last year," Annabelle said, her eyes filled with a sadness I hated seeing in her.

I tried to think back to that time. Van hadn't been himself. He'd been distracted at practice, kept to himself more at home and had been getting drunk more often than I'd ever seen him at any party we hit up. Then he and Annabelle had gotten back together and it was like it had never happened. But I'd never seen him hook up with anyone.

I slung an arm around her shoulders, giving her a reassuring squeeze. "Van cares about you. You have nothing to worry about."

She gave me a small smile. "I hope you're right."

Reaching for her glass, she downed the rest of her drink.

"You need another one of those?"

She nodded gratefully, and I slid from the booth, taking note of the drink orders the others shouted at my back as I made my way to the bar. Flagging down the bartender, I put in the order, turning to prop my elbows against the counter and survey the crowd while I waited.

It wasn't long before a short blonde in a skin-tight red wrap dress sidled up to me, her tits not-so-subtly brushing my arm.

"Hey West," she said with a flirty smile.

I glanced down at her, and she tipped forward slightly, angling her body so I could see straight down her dress. She had a killer rack, but I forced my eyes up.

Even if Monty and I were only faking, I owed her the respect of playing by the rules. And I wanted to. Because I wanted Monty.

"Hey." I nodded at the girl. "Have we met?"

"I'm Carly, we have body physiology together." She took a sip of her drink, her eyes never leaving me. "I'm hoping we can go back to your place and study."

I raised an eyebrow at her blatant come-on. The old me wouldn't have thought twice about what she was offering. We'd already be in an Uber back to the house.

She placed a hand on my arm and leaned in to whisper in my ear. "I'm a very hands-on study buddy."

Her tongue flicked out, sucking my earlobe into her mouth, and I'd be lying if I said my cock didn't stir behind my zipper. She had a pretty face and a smoking hot body, and I was already three beers down tonight. But I wouldn't do it to Monty. Not when she was the one I really wanted moaning my name.

"Sorry sweetheart," I said, subtly edging away from the girl. "I appreciate everything you're offering, but I'm taken."

She pouted. "Since when?"

The bartender returned with the drinks, and I handed over the cash.

"Since now," I said, balancing the glasses between my fingers. "Hope you find someone to study with."

I made my way back to the table, glancing up to find Imogen and Stella watching me from across the room. Imogen tilted her glass in my direction in salute.

Seems I'd passed the first fake boyfriend test with flying colors.

Chapter Twelve

MONTY

I woke to a crash out in the common room and sat up with a start, my heart hammering in my chest. Had Alec escalated to breaking and entering?

The coffee table screeched across the floor as someone stumbled into it, a drunk Imogen swearing like a sailor.

I blew out a long breath. It was just my idiot best friends.

Stella's laughter echoed through the room, and she shout-whispered at Imogen to keep it down because I was sleeping.

"Not anymore," I said, pulling my door open. "Sounds like your night was..."

I froze.

"West?"

Surprise flooded me, followed by a heady dose of lust as I took him in. He stood by the door, his arms crossed over his chest, an amused smile tugging at the corners of his mouth as he watched Imogen and Stella stumble over each other, their drunken snickers filling the room. He looked mouth-watering in a navy button-down shirt and ripped jeans, and I had to fight the overwhelming urge to throw myself at him.

Get a grip, he's not yours. You're the one who wanted boundaries.

"You can't be mad at us!" Stella said, stumbling over her own feet. "We brought your boyfriend home!"

West's gaze snagged on my pajamas, his expression filling with heat as his eyes roamed my body, taking in my thin black tank top and tiny sleep shorts. "You look... *nice.*"

"Woah," Stella said, staring at West with wide eyes. "I want someone to look at me like that."

If only it were real and not just a fake connection fueled by lust. West only wanted to sleep with me because he couldn't have me. And sure, we could fall into bed together and just about guarantee it would be hot as hell between us if our make-outs were anything to go by. But having sex wasn't the problem. It was everything that went along with sex for me and everything that didn't go along with it for him.

"You know, he's a very loyal fake boyfriend," Imogen said from where she'd sprawled on the couch, careful to keep her head up to stop the room spinning. "Some absolute babe with a body tried to hit on him at the bar."

Stella nodded. "Sucked his ear and everything. It was so hot, I almost got off just watching it."

If I'd thought Tahlia messaging him had been a splinter in my chest, the idea of a beautiful girl throwing herself at West was like a rusty nail to my ribcage.

But I had no right to feel jealous. West wasn't really mine.

If it weren't for me, he'd probably be getting laid right

now with that girl instead of watching my drunk friends stumble around our common room. It didn't mean I was going to sleep with him instead, but his sacrifice wasn't lost on me either.

"I turned her down," West reassured me.

"Yeah, you did!" Imogen said, pointing at him like he'd just scored a winning goal. "Mother fucking fake boyfriend of the year, my friend!" She pushed herself up off the couch, giving me a pointed look. "You should probably blow him to say thank you."

I snorted. "Thanks for the tip," I said, shaking my head at her like an amused mother hen.

Stella offered Imogen a hand and the two of them stumbled off towards their rooms.

"We won't hear a thing!" Stella called over her shoulder. "I'm going to sleep like the dead. Mostly because those tequila shots we did might actually be the death of me."

Imogen groaned. "Oh my God, don't say tequila unless you want me to spew on your shoes."

Their conversation died off as they each shut their respective doors. I'd no doubt find them sprawled on top of their beds in the morning, still fully dressed and complaining about killer headaches.

West shoved his hands in his pockets. "I better go. Just wanted to make sure they got home okay. They were going pretty hard at the bar."

"Thank you for doing that." I gave him a genuine smile. "You really are one of the good ones."

He shrugged. "Don't spread it around. I've spent two years building my scandalous reputation, wouldn't want to blow it now."

I smiled, an awkwardness that had never existed between us falling over the room.

We hadn't seen each other in a week, but we'd been texting. He made me laugh and texting with him had become the perfect antidote to a stressful day of classes and dodging my increasingly relentless ex-boyfriend. From the other side of a phone, it had been easy to forget just how crazy hot West was. But now that he was right in front of me, I was self-conscious and unsure of myself.

"Well, I should go," West said, motioning for the door.

"Wait..." I took a step closer, not wanting him to disappear again. "Stay."

His eyebrows rose in surprise.

"I mean... if you want to," I said, twisting the hem of my tank top.

His returning smile had the tension melting from my body. "I want to. I just wasn't sure if that's something you'd want. You know, boundaries and all that."

I closed the space between us, reaching out to take his hand and towing him to my bedroom. "Wanting you has never been the issue."

Something flickered behind his eyes as I shut the door firmly behind us.

Asking him to stay probably wasn't the smartest decision I'd ever made. I'd spent as much time at my study group resisting the urge to text him as I had actually studying. I'd eventually had to bury my phone in the bottom of my bag to stay focused, a sure sign I was becoming too attached already. But hearing that he'd been loyal in the face of blatant temptation made me want to slide my hands up his muscular chest and kiss him until we were both breathless. It really didn't hurt that he looked like a GQ model and smelled even better.

Instead, I stood awkwardly by my closed door, secretly salivating over the way his shirt stretched over his toned biceps and the way the corner of his mouth hitched as he smiled at me.

"You going to stay at least three feet away from me the whole time?" he asked from the end of my bed. He leaned back on his hands like the poster boy for Calvin Klein and sex appeal. "That'll make it hard to get any sleep."

I moved towards the bed, scooting past him, but he caught my hand. His thumb gently stroked the inside of my wrist, making my pulse spike.

"I'm glad you asked me to stay," he said, his voice low.

We stared at each other for a long moment, the awkwardness from before replaced with a charged kind of energy.

Why was I letting myself get attached to a playboy? It was stupid and reckless and would only lead to disappointment. West couldn't give me what I wanted. He freely acknowledged he wasn't anyone's Mr. Right and everyone's Mr. Right Now.

"Want to watch a movie?" I said, pulling away and reaching for my laptop.

"Sure."

He stood, toeing off his shoes then unbuttoning his shirt and whipping it from his shoulders, leaving him in only his jeans that sat low on his hips and revealing the perfect V that disappeared into his waistband.

I worked hard to swallow. "You should really think about making a permanent switch to shirtless. It works for you."

West chuckled, sliding up the bed and lying back with one arm resting behind his head. He was so tall his feet hung over the end.

"I tried it once in freshman year, walked to all my

classes that way after I lost a bet with some of the guys on the team. The Dean threatened to expel me."

"I think I speak for the entire straight female population on campus when I say the Dean is a total buzzkill."

He chuckled, patting the small section of bed beside him. "Get over here, Quad Girl, let's do this."

I switched off the light, the glow of the laptop filling the room. But I hesitated before climbing onto the bed. We'd *slept* together in West's bed only last week, but tonight felt different. When I'd told him I wanted to stop blurring the lines between us, I had no idea how hard it would be. I wanted him, there was no point in denying it. But wanting him and doing something about it were two different things. I had too much going on with Alec to jump into something new, and sleeping with West would only complicate things even more.

I had to keep my hands to myself and my panties firmly in place.

I flopped down on the bed and his arm came around my shoulders, tucking me to his side. I knew I should pull away and put some space between us, but I couldn't make myself do it. Being in his arms felt way too good. Instead, I propped the laptop between us and pressed play on some Ryan Reynolds action movie.

"I decided not to subject you to a chick flick," I said, tilting my head up to look at him.

"I happen to love a good rom-com so that's a missed opportunity for you, babe."

His gaze dropped to my lips, making my heart pound against my ribcage, torturously aware of all the places our bodies were touching.

Reluctantly, I turned back to the screen, West's arm

tightening around me as we settled in to watch the movie in silence.

Twenty minutes passed before either of us spoke.

"Forget three-pointers or NBA finals," West said, his voice husky in the dark. "These shorts you're wearing are my new favorite thing."

Is that what he'd been thinking about this whole time? Not that I could talk. I'd been lying here quietly dreaming about running my hands over his abs, just like I'd wanted to that morning in his bed.

He rolled on his side so we were facing each other, his arm still behind my head while his free hand trailed up my thigh to the hem of my shorts. His fingers grazed the underside of my ass before gliding back down again, goosebumps breaking out over my skin.

"I missed you," he said in a low voice, his face lit only by the glow of the laptop in my dark dorm room.

He trailed soft fingers up and down my thigh, staring at me like he wanted to be my whole world.

"It's only been a week," I said, smoothing my hand over his pec and shoulder. The feel of his warm skin—and the notion I was touching him at all—was exhilarating. "But I missed you too."

His fingers left my thigh to close over my hip, tugging me against him and my body lit up like a Christmas tree at his touch, nervous energy humming through my veins.

The two of us were like magnets, inexplicably drawn to each other, snapping together with overwhelming need.

"Monty..." His hand glided over my hip to slide up my back, fingers tangling in my hair at the base of my neck. "I want you to know that I respect everything you've said about boundaries."

I swallowed, caught up in the intensity of those blue eyes. "But?"

He smiled, slow and seductive. "But I really want to kiss you right now."

My core clenched with heat, and I gave the slightest arch of my back, our bodies pressing closer, West's hand tightened in my hair.

"I can't stop thinking about you," he breathed. "Stella and Imogen getting wasted was great for me because it meant I'd get to see you."

I melted into him at his sweet words, and his mouth inched closer to mine.

Kissing would be the exact opposite of not blurring the lines between us, but nothing in me wanted to stop. I'd wanted to feel his hands on me the moment I'd seen him standing in the common room. He wanted it too if the hard length of him against my hip was anything to go by.

"You're so beautiful," West murmured in the dark.

His breath was warm against my mouth, only an inch of space between our lips...

A crash filled the room, my window shattering all over the floor along with a loud thump against the carpet, and West and I jolted apart.

"What the fuck..." West said, his arms tightening protectively around me as we both sat up.

I stared at my broken window, then at the rock sitting in the middle of the floor.

Scrambling to my feet on the bed and gripping the bedhead, I leaned over to peer out into the darkness. Our dorm was on the ground floor, only separated from the walkway by a small garden bed. It would be so easy to throw something and bolt.

"Did someone just throw a fucking rock through your

window?" West asked, standing on the bed and leaning over the top of me, eyes scanning the path.

It was still and silent.

"They're already gone," I said, turning to stare at the mess on my floor. "Why would someone do that?"

Someone had just *vandalized* my room. The thought made my stomach churn.

"Monty? Is everything okay?" came Stella's voice through the door. "Can we come in?"

"Yeah, we're decent."

West gave me a pointed look and motioned to his bare abs. "Speak for yourself. I was saving this view for my future wife. I was making a generous exception for you."

I gave him a playful shove, but his banter took the edge off my panic.

The door opened and Imogen and Stella appeared, looking disheveled and still drunk. I'm surprised they'd woken at all.

"Wow, Romeo, you certainly fuck hard," Imogen said, taking in the mess.

I crawled to the end of my bed to grab my slipper boots. "It wasn't him."

"First of all, I do fuck hard," West said, sitting on my mattress and leaning against the wall. "But this wasn't me. Some asshole threw a rock through Monty's window."

"What the hell..." Stella said, eyes wide as she glanced between the window and the mess on the floor. A cool breeze blew through, chilling the room.

I slid from the end of the bed to avoid the broken glass and headed for my closet, pulling on a sweatshirt.

West levelled me with a look. "You can't be serious with that sweatshirt, babe."

I glanced down. The words *Pierson Football* were

emblazoned across my chest. One of Imogen's hook-ups had left it behind, and I'd snagged it for my own.

"Is now really the time to get territorial?" I asked.

"You want to get all caveman," Imogen said. "Why don't you get worked up about whoever just tried to throw a rock at your girlfriend."

West sat up. "Do you even need to ask? We know who did this."

I glanced at Imogen and Stella, their worried looks no doubt a mirror for my own.

Would Alec really throw a rock through my window? With the way his behavior had been escalating lately, if he'd seen West come in here, it was possible. But did I really believe he was permanently camped outside my dorm watching my every move? It seemed unlikely.

"I don't know..." I said, mostly because I didn't want it to be true.

All three of them stared back at me in disbelief.

"Do you really think someone would throw a rock through your window as some kind of random prank?" Stella said.

I shrugged, not willing to admit the truth. That if they were right, there really was only one person this could be, but that meant he'd escalated to property damage along with stalking and obsessive texting.

West ran a hand through his hair. "Monty, come on."

"It has to be him," Imogen said.

I sighed, the gravity of the situation landing on me like a weight.

"I guess it's time to go to the campus police."

Chapter Thirteen

WEST

How'd it go, babe?

It was Friday afternoon, and I was on the bus with the team on the way to Kensington State for an away game. It was only a forty-five-minute ride, but I'd spent most of it thinking about Monty when I should have been thinking about how to keep our five-and-one win ratio.

I'd offered to go with her to report Alec and his shady bullshit to campus police. It would have meant I missed the team bus to the game, but I didn't care. Coach would have let me drive myself for something as important as that.

But she'd told me she'd be fine with Stella and Imogen, and she'd see me later at the game. She had planned to come watch me play, catching a ride with Annabelle and her friend later tonight.

Not great. They said they'd talk to

Alec, but there wasn't much they
could do. It was kind of humiliating.

I sat up straighter in my seat, tapping out a response. I hated the creep for making her feel unsafe.

Nothing to be humiliated about, babe.
Alec is the one acting like an insane
asshole.
You don't have to come to the game
tonight if you're not up for it.

Her reply was immediate.

No way! I can't wait to see you
play x

"Who's got you smiling like that?" Davis said from across the aisle.

"None of your damn business."

He smirked. "Hope it's your girlfriend. Or are you back to your old dirty dog ways already?"

I shot him a hard look. "Still with Monty. We can't all make out with topless babes in the kitchen for the rest of our lives."

His grin spread wide with pride. "I'm happy to carry that torch for the house for as long as it's needed."

"I'm not sure we ever needed it," Van said from the row behind me, and I chuckled.

He got up, taking the spare seat beside me. "What's going on with you and Monty? You didn't come home last night."

"Sorry, Mom. Did you wait up for me?"

"You know what I mean. You're into her, whether you want to admit it or not. So why are you still only pretending to be with her?"

I scrubbed a hand over my face. "Sure, I like her. But you know how I feel about relationships. My parents ruined those for me for life. And if I get drafted to the NBA, I'm gone. Besides, Monty has made it pretty clear she isn't interested in anything more than what we already have going on."

"Looked like she was pretty into you at the frat party."

I shrugged. "I mean, yeah, we're attracted to each other, but she won't let it go any further than that. She's still got a lot of fucked up shit going on with her ex."

He frowned. "The guy from the quad?"

I nodded. "He tossed a rock through her window last night when I was there."

His eyes widened. "Were Stella and Imogen home?"

I slid my gaze to him. I tell him someone threw a rock through Monty's window and that's his first question?

"What?" he asked, face a picture of innocence. "It was a good thing you were there, is what I mean. Would have been hell for Monty if her roommates had been out and she was alone when it happened."

"Yeah, I'm glad we were all there, too. The guy is psychotic."

I ran a hand through my hair. I was already way more into her than I should be, given the short time we'd known each other. But I couldn't stop thinking about her. She was smart and sweet and beautiful, and for the first time I couldn't have exactly what I wanted when I wanted it. Monty was a smokeshow who'd held my attention for longer than any girl had since I came to Pierson. And right now, there was no other bed I was interested in being in but hers.

It had been so long since a girl had actually made me work for her attention.

That had to be it.

It wasn't like it was anything more.

Chapter Fourteen

MONTY

Pierson were down by three in the dying minutes of the last quarter and the crowd in the packed stadium was deafening. I stomped my feet and clapped right along with them, my heart pounding in my chest as Kensington took the ball.

The Kensington player went for a high pass across the key to his teammate, but Van was fast, jumping for the intercept. He rocketed down the court with the ball, Annabelle and her friend Laina screaming their heads off as he passed it off to Chen, who put it in for a lay-up, sending the Pierson side of the stadium into a frenzy.

We were down by one, and Kensington had the ball.

West pushed up court to meet the player head on, the guy trying to dodge around him, but West was too fast, predicting it and going with him every time he tried to make a move.

They edged down the court together, West staying on him, waiting for the perfect opening.

Frustration peaking, the Kensington player stepped back, trying for a three-point shot from way off the key, but West snatched the shot from the air before it could sail anywhere close to the ring.

The crowd erupted in approval, West pounding down the court with the ball, Hernandez and Williams at his heels. He stopped short of the three-point line, putting up a beautiful arching shot that sailed into the hoop right on the buzzer.

"Oh my fucking god, they won!" Annabelle said, her eyes wide.

She wrapped me in a hug, jumping up and down, the Pierson crowd losing their minds at our team snatching victory in the dying seconds.

Pierson players swarmed West, hugging and shoving him until he was buried in a mass of bodies. The stands vibrated and cheerleaders bounced around the huddle of players like energized dolls.

You'd think Pierson had just won the championship game from the way we were celebrating, but even I couldn't deny the buzzing high of the win coursing through me.

The Kensington players ambled off the court with heads hanging. I *almost* felt sorry for them. Being beaten on the buzzer in their own house had to hurt.

When the Pierson players finally let West go, he jogged across the court, climbing the few steps of the stands to where I stood on the end of the row. His face was flushed, his chest heaving from the exertion of the game, those blue eyes sparkling from the adrenaline of victory.

Without a word, his hand curled around my waist, the other one sliding along my jaw, his mouth closing over mine. Heat seared through my veins as our tongues swept over each other in slow, purposeful strokes.

95

Forget boundaries. He can kiss me whenever he wants as long as he does it exactly like this.

The crowd cheered around us, and West pulled away, a panty-melting grin spreading across his stupidly hot face.

Then he bounded down the steps to join his teammates.

"Wow," Annabelle said, eyes wide. "That was so hot. Now I know what Adam means about you two."

Heat crept into my cheeks. "I can't believe he just did that."

"Me either," Laina said. "I've never seen West act like that. You're so lucky."

We'd ignored the rules and crossed a line. But surely celebrating West taking the winning shot in a nail-biter was an exception?

At least that's what I tried to tell myself.

Chapter Fifteen

WEST

I messaged Monty and asked her to wait for me after the game. Coach had pulled me aside in the locker room for a pep talk about how great I was—at least that's what I'd taken from it—which meant once I'd showered and changed, I was one of the last ones out.

Monty was waiting for me at the end of the tunnel, the stadium mostly empty except for a few Kensington stragglers.

"Hey, is everything okay?" she asked as I approached, her eyes scanning me in concern.

I scooped her into my arms. "Yeah, we just won. Why wouldn't everything be okay?"

She tilted her head, levelling me with a flat stare. "When you asked me to meet you outside the locker room, I thought something had happened. Annabelle and Laina are waiting for me to drive back to Pierson."

"Text them, tell them you're getting a ride back with me."

She pulled a face. "Didn't you take the team bus?"

"I did."

"So, your coach is fine with you bringing people on with you?"

A smile spread across my face at her innocence. "No. I'm going to sneak you on."

She stared back at me, debating it in her mind.

"Fine, but if I get caught, you're taking the fall. Coach Sorensen is intense, I don't want his rage directed at me."

She pulled out her phone, composing a text to Annabelle, while I stood there drinking her in. I couldn't believe we'd snatched the win tonight and I was buzzing that Monty had been here to see it. If it were my choice, I knew exactly how I wanted to celebrate with her, but I'd already crossed a line when I'd kissed her. Keeping my hands to myself was proving harder than I expected. Especially when she was standing there looking hot as fuck in tight jeans that hugged her ass and waist, and a navy and white Pierson Basketball t-shirt that I was almost certain if she turned around would have my name and jersey number on the back.

My hands closed over her waist, spinning her, and she let out a squeak of surprise, eyes still trained on her phone. And call me a fucking caveman, but the sight of my name across her shoulders made my goddamn dick stir in my sweats.

"You look so hot, babe."

I wanted to drag her into the locker room and go down on her until she moaned my name. But that particular fantasy wasn't going to happen any time soon.

Boundaries.

She glanced up, eyeing me with suspicion at whatever

expression she read on my face. But before she had a chance to say anything, someone called my name.

"West Wright?" said a tall middle-aged man with thick glasses and brown hair that was greying at the temples. "I'm Corey Edmond, scout for Philadelphia."

He offered me his hand, and I took it. His handshake was firm but friendly.

"Pleasure to meet you, sir."

Monty's gaze darted between me and Mr. Edmond.

"I wanted to come and introduce myself and congratulate you on a great game tonight, son."

I schooled my expression, not wanting to reveal just how amped I was to hear an NBA scout had not only seen me play, but was praising my performance.

"Thank you, sir."

"Given the team's current scoring record, I'm looking forward to seeing you play in the Pierson game against Minnesota in a few weeks. We've certainly got our eye on you." He gave me a wink like we were old buddies.

"Looking forward to it, sir. I hope we can make it worth the trip."

"I'm sure you will." He glanced at Monty, smiling at us both. "You kids have a good night."

Without waiting for a response, he turned and strode across the court, leaving me staring after him.

"Oh, I'm sorry..." Monty said, looking awed. "Is someone getting recruited to the NBA?"

I laughed, surprise at Mr. Edmond's introduction still coursing through me. "I wouldn't go that far."

She smacked me in the shoulder. "I would. That guy is half in love with your skills already!"

I shook my head, refusing to get ahead of myself. Scouts

came to watch college games all the time. Just because Edmond said Philly had their eye on me tonight didn't mean they still would in a week. It was all dependent on performance. Not just my own, but everyone else playing college ball across the country. Coach had spent the past two years drilling into us how fickle scouts could be about their favorites.

All I could control was my game when I hit the court.

"You'd be half in love with my skills too if you let us ditch your rules," I said, throwing an arm around her shoulders.

It was so damn cute the way her cheeks flooded with heat at the suggestion.

She rolled her eyes and slung an arm around my back to steady us as we trailed across the court. "Whatever, superstar. Annabelle just left, so if I don't make it onto this bus, I guess I go to Kensington now."

"Why would you want to side with the losing team? Especially since Pierson players are not only winners, but so much better looking. I hear they're better in bed too."

She shrugged. "Oh, I don't know. Number six for Kensington had some killer calves and a sweet jump shot."

I knew she was joking, but it didn't stop the stab of white-hot jealousy that seared through me.

"Better than these bad boys?" I cocked a leg out, twisting it so she could admire the view. "Tell me you've seen sexier calves, and I'll show you a liar."

She wrinkled her nose. "Eh."

I was about to berate her for questioning my sporting prowess when Williams called out from the doorway.

"Wright! Bus is leaving, let's go."

I pulled a hooded sweatshirt from my sports bag and handed it to Monty. "Put this on and pull it up."

She'd blend in with the rest of the guys in a team sweatshirt; I just had to hope nobody glanced down at her amazing ass in those jeans.

She sure as hell didn't look like any teammate I'd ever had.

Taking her hand in mine, I led her out of the stadium, the bus idling near the door.

Coach was still outside, deep in conversation with one of the defensive coaches, and I walked straight for the bus, climbing aboard with Monty in tow.

Most of the boys didn't even look up, some with headphones in or already asleep, too wiped from the game to care. But a few whistles went up as we made our way down the aisle to the back where Bant, Van and Davis were waiting.

"So, you score the winning shot and now suddenly you're a badass?" Davis asked, nodding his head at Monty. "Sup, Quad Girl?"

She grinned from inside the hood of my sweatshirt. If I didn't already know what a superfan she was of rules, I'd say breaking them gave her a thrill.

I stepped aside so she could slide into the window seat in the second last row. Davis was in front of us, Van was already asleep across the aisle.

Bant hung over the back of the chair. "Keep that hood up, Monts, and Coach will never know."

We bumped fists and he slid back into his seat as Coach climbed aboard.

"Listen up, boys," he called, eyes roaming over us. Monty ducked lower. "We've got just shy of an hour's drive back to Pierson and after tonight's performance, you've earned yourselves the break."

The bus filled with whistles and cheers.

"When we get back to campus, I know you're going to

want to celebrate. Don't go overboard because tomorrow we get back to work."

Coach took his seat to a chorus of whistles and shouts, the bus rumbling beneath us as it pulled away from the Kensington stadium.

"So..." Monty said. "What do you guys usually do on these bus rides?"

"Watch porn and jerk each other off," Davis said with a straight face.

I shoved the back of his chair and he slid down in his seat, chuckling.

"Sleep, mostly," Van added, without opening his eyes.

Turning to her, I lowered my voice. "We can do anything you want."

Those grey-blue eyes lit up. "Anything?"

I quirked an eyebrow. "What did you have in mind?"

"Something really sexy."

I knew she was probably messing with me, getting me to think she wanted to ride me in the back of the bus. But my dick didn't care because he wanted it to be true. Monty was sexy as hell, but especially when she got that spark in her eyes when she messed with me.

"Oh, yeah? What's that?" I asked, closing the space between us.

"Watching *Riverdale* on Netflix on your phone."

I burst out a laugh, Davis throwing us a look over his shoulder between the seats.

"You got it, babe." I pulled my air pods from my sweat-shirt pocket and handed one over, then queued up my phone.

Monty snuggled into me.

The team had won after I'd sunk the final ball, a scout

had told me I was on his radar, and now I had Monty tucked under my arm for the entire ride back to school.

I was one lucky son of a bitch.

* * *

We made it back to campus in record time. Bant, Van and Davis helping me sneak Monty off the bus without drawing attention from Coach.

The five of us piled into my car.

"You crashing at our place tonight, Quad Girl?" Van asked from the front seat.

Monty, who was squeezed in the back between Bant and Davis, glanced at me in the rearview mirror.

"Yeah, I mean... if that's okay."

When we'd tried for a sleepover before it had been interrupted by a rock coming through her window. I was definitely up for round two, minus the drama. Even if sex was off the table, I was happy to sleep with Monty's warm body tucked to my side, the scent of her in my bed.

I winked at her. "I want you there, babe."

Van turned in his seat to face her, putting on his most innocent expression. "I want you there too, babe."

Davis rolled his head in her direction like the dramatic dickhead he was. "Don't forget me, babe. I want you there too."

"I want you there, babe," Bant said, throwing an arm around her and hitting Davis in the eye.

"Ow, for fuck's sake, Bant," Davis said, clutching his face.

"Bro, it was an accident, and I really didn't hit you that hard. Stop being such a baby."

When I glanced back at Monty, her lips were pressed together, fighting a laugh.

"Monty, I'm injured," Davis whined. "Got any hot friends who can come over and kiss it better?"

"All of Monty's friends are hot," Van said, staring out at the road ahead of us.

Bant whacked him on the back of the head. "Eyes on the prize, dickhead. You've got a girlfriend."

"I'm taken, not dead. I can still appreciate hot women when I see them."

"Like how hot are we talking?" Davis asked.

Monty screwed up her nose. "Those are my friends, don't talk about them like they're walking fun bags for you to play with."

The car fell silent.

"Anyone else just thinking about tits now that Monty said fun bags?" Davis asked.

All four of us raised our hands, Monty's melodic laugh filling the car.

Chapter Sixteen

MONTY

"How's the story coming along, word wizard?"

I glanced up from my table in the middle of the cavernous library to find West grinning down at me, two cups of coffee in his hands.

"Horribly. There are plot holes everywhere, and I keep hoping someone else will come along and magically fill them for me," I whispered, glancing at the students nearby to make sure they weren't shooting us daggers for talking in such a sacred space.

He slid into the chair across from me. "Yeah, I can't help with that. But I brought caffeine to keep you going. Aren't I a thoughtful boyfriend?"

He'd taken to using that word a lot the past few weeks and I had no idea what to make of it. So just like every other time, I ignored it and pretended like it was nothing.

But it was definitely something.

I motioned to the coffees. "You know you could get

kicked out for bringing that kind of hardcore contraband into the library, rulebreaker."

He waggled his eyebrows at me. "It's fun to break the rules. We should try it together sometime. Preferably between my sheets."

He'd been doing more of that too—bringing up the idea of us sleeping together. We hadn't kissed since he'd laid one on me in the heat of victory after the Kensington game, but something had definitely shifted between us. We were more affectionate and relaxed with one another, falling into our fake relationship with real gusto.

Some days it was all too easy to forget we weren't actually together. Especially when he'd invite me over to watch movies with the guys, or text me about my day, or turn up to the library with coffee to fuel my study sessions. It was becoming more and more difficult to guard my swooning heart from his charm.

"I'll have to take your word for it. I'm more of a law-abiding kind of girl," I said, turning back to my laptop.

He leaned across the table, keeping his voice low. "You definitely got a thrill from sneaking on the team bus, don't even try to deny it."

I pressed my lips together knowing there was no point lying.

"Fine, breaking the rules was fun then, but I happen to like coming here. It's usually peaceful." I gave him a pointed look. "And I don't want you getting me kicked out permanently because you spilled coffee all over some ancient, irreplaceable book."

He raised his hands innocently. "I promise the only place the coffee goes is in my mouth."

My gaze dropped to that perfect mouth, remembering the feel of those lips on mine. God, I was becoming way too addicted to him, and we hadn't even slept together. Not for lack of trying on his part.

West's expression hardened as he stared over my right shoulder. "Do you know Alec's here?"

"Yeah, he came in about five minutes after me and sat over there."

West's concerned gaze cut back to me. "Has he come over here?"

I shook my head. "Hasn't even wandered by."

West's eyes narrowed. "I don't like it."

Reaching out, I covered his hand with mine where it rested on the table and the rigid set of his shoulders softened slightly.

"He hasn't done anything, I'm fine." I shrugged, going back to my laptop again. "Maybe he's finally moving on."

Doubt lingered on West's face, and I didn't have the heart to admit that Alec's lurking made me more uneasy than a direct approach. But it was true that Alec hadn't bothered me since we'd both arrived, and I'd somehow managed to put him out of my mind.

"I have to get back to work, this story submission isn't going to write itself."

West reached into his backpack and pulled out his own laptop and notebook.

"Don't mind me, I'm just here to be the best study buddy you've ever had." He grinned at me and the urge to reach over the table and kiss him hit me so hard it physically pained me to resist.

Why did he have to be so ridiculously attractive?

"What?" An amused frown creased his forehead, his eyes alight with understanding.

I shook my head. "Nothing."

"I know I'm a fine piece of ass, but try to keep your

drool in your mouth, Monty. This is a library, not a sex club, you menace."

A laugh burst out of me in the hushed silence. "Can't make any promises."

We spent the next hour in silence, studying on our respective laptops. Until West tossed his pen down on his notebook.

"Damn it, I can't remember the name of like eight different muscles, and I didn't bring my textbook. Hopefully they have a copy here."

He pushed to his feet, his chair scraping in the silence.

"Wow, I never thought you'd have trouble with body parts," I said, biting down on my teasing smile.

West halted, leaning down so close his lips brushed my ear and sending a delicious shiver shooting down my back.

"Follow me into the stacks, and I'll show you how great I am with different parts of your body," he said, his husky voice making my thighs clench.

He didn't wait for a response, sauntering through the tables of studying students, girls glancing up from their textbooks to watch him go.

I didn't blame them. His firm ass and muscular legs looked incredible in those basketball sweats, and I didn't need to see his rock-hard abs to know that's what was hiding beneath his hooded sweatshirt.

My god, I wanted him so badly. I was having a hard time remembering why I'd ever wanted boundaries between us.

What would happen if I followed him into the stacks? Would we really go at it against the books where anyone could walk by? Knowing West, he'd probably already done it at least twice.

I went to turn back around, my gaze landing on Alec,

who was watching me. A shiver of unease ran through me, and I turned away. It felt like I'd been caught out doing something I shouldn't, but if I wanted to check out my fake boyfriend's ass, I would. Alec didn't get to make me feel any kind of way for moving on.

Engrossed in my work, it took me twenty-five minutes to notice that West hadn't returned. He wasn't seriously holding out for me to come join him, was he?

Shutting both our laptops, I slid them into my bag, pushing them under the desk. Then I slipped between the tables, going deeper into the library. I passed row after row of shelves, my head darting back and forth down the aisles like I was watching a tennis match as I searched each section for West. I'd made it almost halfway down the main aisle when a flirtatious giggle echoed through the stacks.

Rounding the end of the next aisle I found West halfway down and he wasn't alone.

He was pressed against the shelf, a short curvy redhead in a cheerleader's outfit invading his space. His expression appeared friendly enough, but there was an uncomfortable pinch to his brow.

Since when was West Wright anything but charming around women?

The cheerleader trailed a seductive finger from his pec to his abs, shifting closer. West stared down at her finger, giving her a tight smile.

A protectiveness flared inside me and before I knew what I was doing, I was stalking toward them.

West's eyes widened as he saw me. "Monty, I…"

I slid my arms around his neck, sliding my body against him. "Here you are, babe. I've been looking everywhere for you."

Without waiting for his reply, I pressed my mouth to

his, kissing him long and slow. My tongue swept over his in lazy strokes, my fingers running over the back of his head. I arched my back, my hips grinding closer, and my chest pressed against him.

When I pulled away, he blinked several times, then a wide grin spread across his face, his blue eyes sparking.

"Monty, this is Gina." West motioned to the cheer-leader, and I turned my head, keeping my arms wrapped around him. "This is my girlfriend, Monty."

I smiled at Gina, ignoring the tug in my stomach at hearing West introduce me that way.

The girl narrowed her eyes. "I heard a rumor you had a girlfriend, but I didn't believe it."

I shrugged, answering for him. "Well, here I am."

Turning back to West, I gripped the back of his head and tugged his mouth to mine again. The moment our lips touched a bolt of electricity skittered through me.

Holy hell. I'd forgotten exactly what I was missing when I'd slapped that kissing ban on us. He'd kissed me at the game, and it had been a spark in the night. But it had been short and sweet, and I'd been too focused on the fact I was caught up in such a public display of affection to really enjoy it.

But this kiss? This kiss was Fourth of July fireworks.

West's hands closed over my hips, caressing me like he was worried I might spook at any second and pull away so he needed to get his fill now. The way he used his tongue should be illegal, sweeping over mine and sending a jolt of heat straight to my core.

I let out a small moan and Little Miss Cheerleader made a disgruntled noise behind me, her footsteps fading as she stalked off.

West pulled away, shooting me a grin. "Thanks for saving me."

"Mmhmm, you're welcome. I'm not done," I said, pulling his lips back to mine.

He smiled against my mouth, arms wrapping around my waist, one hand dipping to cup my ass.

We kissed until we were both breathless, my lips plump and swollen and heat well and truly pooling between my legs from his skillful touch and even more skillful tongue.

"Does this mean the kissing ban is over?" he asked, eyes twinkling with a mix of desire and amusement.

I pushed up on my toes, kissing along his jaw and enjoying the jolt of pleasure that ran through him. Now that I'd crossed the line, I couldn't keep my hands off him.

"Screw the kissing ban," I said, nipping at his ear with my teeth.

He gripped my ass with both hands, spinning us around so I was the one pressed against the shelves.

"Well, thank fuck for that."

* * *

West partially got his wish, given we spent fifteen minutes making out in the stacks. When we eventually made it back to our table looking slightly more disheveled than when we'd left, the library had mostly emptied.

"Gosh, don't you hate it when your former conquest accosts you in the library when you're trying to study?" I teased, as we packed up our stuff.

West raised an eyebrow. "As opposed to the stalker ex who shows up everywhere you go?"

"Touché, Big Man."

He laughed, taking his laptop back. "Big Man? That's new. And you haven't even seen me naked yet." He winked.

I swung my backpack on and West threw an arm around my shoulders, guiding us to the door. Tucked under his arm had fast become one of my favorite places to be.

We wandered out into the cold night air, West pulling up short to stare at something.

"Everything okay?" I asked.

He motioned to the ornate stone lion statues sitting on either side of the doorway to the library. "Some girl once said kissing me was like making out with one of those."

I frowned, trying to hide my smile. "Hmm, that's quite the insult."

His gaze narrowed on me.

"The silly bitch didn't know what she was talking about," I said, waving his worries away. "Your lips are softer than a cloud, and she clearly had no idea about all the insane things you could do with your tongue."

West smiled like a kid at Christmas. "That's more like it." He pressed a kiss to the top of my head. "But call my girlfriend a bitch again and you and I are going to have a serious problem."

I laughed, the two of us walking through campus towards West's car, wrapped around each other in the growing twilight. I no longer cared if this relationship had started out as fake, because the connection we were building felt so real. And maybe I was a fool for letting myself believe it, but maybe there was a chance West and I could really be something. So long as I could finally get rid of Alec first.

Twenty-five minutes later we were in the living room at the basketball house, Bant and Reggie engrossed in the NBA game they were playing on the PlayStation, Hernandez, Van, Davis, West and I lounging around eating pizza while we watched.

Chen was in his room cramming for a mid-term, Jericho had been dragged to his girlfriend's dance recital and the guys said Williams was out with his girlfriend.

"What do you think of this girl I'm trying to bone?" Davis asked, brandishing a photo on his phone. "She's cute as fuck, right?"

"Is she cute or is she just wearing a really short skirt?" Hernandez asked, slouching back on the couch with a slice of pizza in one hand and a beer in the other.

"Says the guy with the supermodel girlfriend," Bant said with a snort, his eyes never leaving the screen.

It was true. I'd met Hernandez's girlfriend, Harley, at one of the guys' games and she was stunning. All long legs, smooth dark skin and enormous brown eyes. She was studying psychology like Imogen, but she booked modelling jobs part time. She'd shown me a picture of her in Calvin Klein underwear on a billboard in Times Square.

"I don't care about the skirt, just what's under it," Davis said. "I'm telling her to come over."

I scowled. "Way to be a gentleman, Davis. Do you even know her name?"

He paused in his typing, eyes sliding to me. "Sure, I do."

Everyone fell quiet, save for the mashing of PlayStation controllers and the overexcited commentator narrating the game through the screen.

"Well?" West asked.

Davis shifted in his seat. "It's like Susie or Stacey or something."

A communal groan went up. Van tossed a bottle cap at Davis, and it bounced off his head.

"Whatever," Davis said. "I'm still inviting her over."

"I hope if she agrees you show her more than just your bedroom," I said, reaching for a slice of pepperoni. "Ask her if she wants some pizza, offer her a drink. Do a little more than just trying to get into her pants."

He didn't even glance up from his typing. "Only for you, Quad Girl."

"Monty doesn't want you fucking in her honor, D. Get over yourself," Bant said, staring at the game on the TV screen.

"Jeez, what crawled up your ass tonight?" Reggie asked, dunking over Bant's player and earning himself a high score.

Bant swore and threw the controller on the table. He picked up his beer and Hernandez picked up the controller to take over.

"He can't get the girl he wants," Van said with a snort.

Bant scowled. "Shut the hell up."

He pulled his phone from his pocket, unlocked it and showed me a text chain.

"Her name's Cleo, she's in my econ class. I know she's interested because she flirts with me constantly, but whenever I ask her to hang out, she shuts me down."

"A lady killer like you? Surely not," I said with a teasing smile, remembering the hard time Imogen had given him at the frat party.

Bant sat back on the couch with a groan. "She's ruining my scoring average."

"First of all, do you care about her or just your scoring average? Because I'm not going to help you if all you care about is getting your dick wet and not the actual girl it's with."

Bant's gaze slid to me. "I mean, obviously I want to get laid. But I do like this girl. If she wanted to make it a regular thing, I wouldn't be opposed."

I pulled a face. "How romantic. I can't understand why she's not falling at your feet."

Bant groaned again, throwing an arm over his eyes, and completely missing my sarcasm. "I know, I don't get it either. Clearly my game is slipping. You've got to help me, Monty."

I scanned the text messages between them.

"Seems to me that she's interested but hesitant."

West's arm came around me and he leaned in to read the messages over my shoulder. I relaxed against him, relishing the delicious heat of his body.

"You need to tell her you like her. Make her feel special. Why do you want to hang out with her over any other girl?"

Bant lowered his arm. "Because she's hot as fuck. Shouldn't that be obvious?"

Davis nodded in agreement, face innocent like a schoolboy looking for praise. "Women like to know they're more than just a nice ass and a good pair of tits, right, Monty?"

I pressed my lips together to keep from laughing. "You're right. Women like to feel special."

"That how West scored you?" Reggie asked, waggling his eyebrows.

"No, he showed me his jump shot, then his giant dick," I said, deadpan.

Reggie fumbled the controller, letting Hernandez score. West laughed, his thumb gliding back and forth over my shoulder with casual ease.

Bant sat up. "Can't I just do that with Cleo? My jump shot is the best on the team."

The other guys howled him down.

I patted his knee. "No. You're going to have to put in a little effort."

He took his phone back and sat with his elbows on his knees, texting furiously.

The night and the conversation moved on, leaving Davis and Bant's girl problems behind.

Half an hour later the doorbell rang, and Davis sprang to his feet. "I'll get it!"

He opened the front door, his eyes widening in dumbfounded delight as a sophomore in tight jeans and a cute blue tank stepped inside, sliding her coat from her shoulders.

It was way too cold out for just a tank and coat, but I understood the play she was making. She looked incredible. Clearly Davis thought so too, given the way his tongue was hanging out of his mouth, his eyes tracking every move she made.

"Hi, I'm Sarah," she said, with a little wave, and I resisted the urge to roll my eyes at Davis claiming her name was Stacey or Susie.

Everyone introduced themselves and Davis led Sarah to the armchair he'd been sitting in. "Take a seat, can I get you a drink?"

Sarah smiled up at him. "A beer would be great, thanks."

When he turned to the kitchen, he shot me a wink.

"Tell me," West said quietly, lips brushing my ear. "What are you going to do when every girl on campus wants to murder you because they fell for Davis's charm? You've turned him into a wooing weapon."

"Murder me? They'll be thanking me for teaching him the bare minimum of what a guy should do. You jocks have it way too easy."

West chuckled and my stomach tightened at the sound. Even his laugh made me want him.

"What was it you called me at that frat party? Mr. Hump and Dump? That's Davis and you've just taught him what chivalry is. Girls all across campus will be coming for you."

I snuggled closer under his arm, angling my body towards his.

"If they're stupid enough to believe a word that comes out of that boy's mouth and fall into bed with him anyway, they have no one to blame but themselves."

He grinned, hooking a finger under my chin and tilting my face towards him. My heart stuttered in my chest, remembering the taste of his lips in the library.

"You have no idea how badly I want to kiss you right now," West said.

I stared back at him, his intense expression making me nervous. I slowly shook my head.

West's eyes narrowed. "You said the kissing ban was done."

"You're right, I did say that. But I'm not looking for some public PDA in front of your teammates."

He pulled a face. "You literally jumped me in the quad in front of Bant and Van."

I laughed. "Okay, but that's different."

He raised an eyebrow. "How?"

I leaned in to whisper in his ear. "Because now that there are no rules or boundaries between us, we don't want to start something we can't finish in a packed room."

West groaned, his head falling to the back of the couch. "You're killing me."

"You two are so cute together," Sarah said with a smile. "How long have you been dating?"

I patted West on the knee. "He's been chasing me for a

while, but I only finally gave in to him a few months ago. Lucky guy."

West smiled and shook his head at me, and Davis returned with Sarah's drink.

"You want to stay down here and have some pizza or you want to go hang in my room?"

Sarah got to her feet, her eyes trailing over his muscular basketball body. "Let's go hang out in your room."

Davis fist pumped the air behind Sarah's back as they left.

"You've created a monster, Quad Girl," Van said.

West grunted in agreement. "That's what I said."

The doorbell rang again, and we all glanced at each other.

This time Bant jumped up. "My turn."

He pulled the door open, standing aside to let his guest in. "You made it."

A girl with long black hair strolled inside, dressed in black leggings and a fitted black sweater. She had an amazing body and a pretty face. Bant definitely had good taste.

"Cleo, these are the guys." He motioned to me. "And Monty."

I waved, and Cleo waved back.

"Nice to meet you all."

"So..." Bant turned to Cleo. "Can I get you a drink?"

Cleo smiled and nodded. "That would be great."

Bant took her hand and led her to the kitchen.

"Any more of my friends you want to help, or can I have you all to myself now?" West asked.

I smiled up at him. "Well, these three all have girl-friends or boyfriends." I shrugged. "So, I guess I'm all yours."

"Should I break out the Guess Who board or are you happy hanging out with these jokers?"

I glanced at Van, Reggie and Hernandez. If you'd told me at the start of the semester that I'd wind up spending most of my spare time over the next few months at the basketball house I'd have snorted a drink out my nose in disbelief. But now that I was here, you couldn't drag me away. They were a hilariously inappropriate, highly dysfunctional family that I'd somehow become a part of.

"I'm happy here," I said, smiling up at West.

He pressed a kiss to my temple.

"Have you heard about any more scouts coming to your games?" I asked, the sound of the video game and Reggie and Hernandez's trash talking drowning out our conversation.

West shrugged. "There could be one there this week. Then at least two coming to a game against Nebraska in a few weeks."

"So the NBA is it for you? That's the end game?"

He glanced down at me, expression serious. "It's been the goal for as long as I can remember. I've never wanted anything as much as I want to make it in the pros."

"You'll get there," I said, and I meant it.

West was magic on the court. He was skilled, unselfish and generally unstoppable.

His expression softened. "Thanks babe, that means a lot."

His gaze dropped to my mouth, and I bit my lip.

"I know what you're thinking..."

The deadliest smile spread across his face, the one that had girls lusting after him all over campus.

"...and I still don't want to make out in a packed living room."

"Not even if I do this?" He leaned in, lips brushing the column of my throat and making me shudder with pleasure.

"Or this?"

His tongue caressed my ear, nipping at it with his teeth, and I bit down on the small groan that threatened to escape.

"I know you want this, babe. I want it too. I love the way your lips part to let me in when I kiss you. The way your tongue slides over mine. I've got a semi just thinking about the feel of your body in my hands."

Our mouths were so close I could feel the warmth of his breath against my skin. Nobody was paying any attention to the two of us huddled together in the corner of the couch.

One little kiss wouldn't hurt...

"I swear to God, you two lock lips in front of me again and I'll get the hose from the yard and hose you both down where you sit," Van said, ruining the moment.

I laughed, pulling away and turning back to the TV.

"This isn't over," West said quietly in my ear.

And I hoped he meant it.

Chapter Seventeen

MONTY

West dropped me back at my dorm, making me promise I'd be at his game tomorrow.

"I play better when you're there, babe," he said, squeezing my knee.

The giddy feeling taking over me was proof of what I'd already come to realize: I was in trouble.

Despite my best attempt at rules and boundaries and not getting too close to him, none of it had stopped West from working his way into my life and my heart.

I was falling for him. And that was a big problem.

West had never given any indication he was interested in anything more than sleeping with me. The moment I showed my growing feelings for him, this fake situationship would be over.

"I'll see you tomorrow, superstar," I said, sliding from the car.

He took off his seatbelt. "Wait, I'll walk you to your door."

"No need, it's right there. I'll be fine."

"Okay, well, text me later. And make sure to have really dirty dreams about me."

I snorted. "I'll get right on that," I said, shutting the door.

Walking down the path towards my dorm, I couldn't wipe the smile off my face.

I was so lost in my own head over West, I didn't notice the person sitting outside my residence hall until I almost tripped right over him.

"Alec, what the hell are you doing here?"

He got to his feet. "Waiting for you."

"Please don't come here. You've got to stop this."

"Stop what? Caring about you? That's never going to happen, Monty. Because I love you and I know you love me too."

Frustration simmered inside me. What was it going to take for him to get it?

"No, I don't love you. I've asked you to stay away from me."

Alec shook his head. "You're only saying these things because *he's* making you."

I screwed up my face. "Who? West? He doesn't make me say or do anything. He's not like that."

"Oh, so it was your idea to make out with him in the library? It was practically pornographic. The Monty I know doesn't do things like that."

I reared back. "You followed me? And you spied on us? Jesus, Alec. You've really lost it."

I went to move past him, but he stepped in front of me.

"I followed you to talk to you. How do you think it made me feel to find you like that with him?"

"Alec, we broke up! Your feelings aren't my responsibility."

I tried to dart around him again into the safety of my dorm, but his hand closed around my wrist and fear jolted in my stomach.

"I love you." He squeezed tight, fingers digging into my flesh. "When are you going to stop this and come back to me?"

I stared into his dark eyes, truly afraid of him for the first time.

"Let me go, Alec." I swallowed. "Now."

A peal of laughter echoed across the campus, a group of students coming down the path, and Alec dropped my arm, stepping away.

"Monty…"

I didn't wait, swiping my way into the building and rushing down the hall to my suite. I slammed the door behind me and fell against it, my heart hammering in my chest so hard I might be sick.

"That's quite an entrance," Stella said from the couch, her smile fading as she took in my expression. She pushed to her feet. "What's happened?"

I shook my head, trying to calm my nerves. "Alec."

"What did he do?"

I walked over to the couch and sat down hard. "He was waiting for me outside. When I tried to go around him, he grabbed me." I glanced at her. "He really scared me, Stell."

Her eyes filled with concern. "Monty, please, you need to report him."

I rubbed my hands over my face, trying to still my hammering heart. "I already did that once and it didn't achieve anything. Alec is still following me and texting me and turning up outside our dorm."

She was quiet for a moment. "Want me to call West?"

I wanted nothing more than to feel West's arms around me right now while he whispered reassuring words in my ear. But I shook my head. Calling him would only make it worse. He'd try to fix it, which would no doubt mean a confrontation with Alec.

And more confrontation was the last thing I needed right now.

Chapter Eighteen

WEST

"Here's to another epic win on the board, boys!"

The entire team knocked their cups together, downing their shots, while the party at the basketball house raged around us.

We'd won again tonight, cementing our eleven-game winning streak. Coach was happy, the team was riding high, and I'd scored twenty-three points in front of a scout for the Rockets.

Monty was across the room talking with Annabelle and Harley and looking like every college guy's dream in a tight black mini skirt that curved perfectly over her ass and plunging black top that showed off her incredible tits. More than a few guys had been eyeing her for most of the night and a raging possessiveness like nothing I'd ever experienced burned through me.

She glanced at her phone for the umpteenth time, frowning down at the screen then ignoring it.

It was Alec texting her. It had to be. No one else would make her brow pinch like that.

I hated that he was still texting her and there was nothing I could do about it. She'd asked me not to interfere, told me to stay away from him. This was her battle to fight, but it didn't mean watching it play out this way didn't grind. The guy needed to take the hint and fuck off.

My teammates huddled around the table, pouring out another round of shots.

"We're out of liquor!" Reggie said to a chorus of boos.

"Alright, alright, keep your shorts on. There's more in the kitchen," I said, slipping past the jersey chasers hovering nearby.

Monty glanced at me as I passed, and I threw her a wink. The small, secret smile that she gave me in return made my chest swell.

What the hell was this feeling she brought out in me? Whatever it was I had no fucking idea what to do with it or how to even broach the idea of changing things between us.

I had swiped a bottle of whiskey from the kitchen counter and was turning back towards the living room when Tahlia sidled up to me, sliding her body against mine.

"West Wright, where the hell have you been lately?" she asked, a seductive smile on her face as she slid her hands up my pecs to wrap them around my neck.

Her familiar scent invaded my senses, dulled from the two rounds of shots I'd already done with the team. She pulled me closer, grinding her hips against my groin.

Jesus.

It had been months since I'd seen any action and here was a near-perfect body rubbing up against me. I may not want her, but it didn't mean I couldn't appreciate how incredible Tahlia's body was. Only it wasn't the body I wanted.

"Tahlia." I tugged one of her arms from around my neck. "I can't..."

"I know you've missed me, baby," she said, cutting me off and running a hand over my hair. "Sometimes I think about you when I'm in bed all alone."

She pressed up on her toes, her lips brushing my ear.

"I think about all the times we hooked up while I touch myself."

My jaw clenched and I tried to pull away.

"Seriously, Tahlia. I appreciate it, but I can't..."

Before I could get another word out, her mouth closed over mine, trapping my lips against her. Her mouth was warm and soft, and while it should have felt familiar, it was all wrong.

I'd barely had time to register what her lips on mine meant when Davis's voice boomed through the kitchen.

"Pay up, Hernandez! I knew he wasn't a one-woman kind of guy. Oh shit, sorry Monty."

I pushed Tahlia away, gaze darting to Monty standing in the doorway, hurt and betrayal flashing in those grey-blue eyes.

"If I was going to become a one-woman man for anyone, it'd be you, sweetheart," Davis said, trying to comfort her in his own useless way.

I was across the kitchen in a heartbeat, reaching for her. "Monty, that wasn't me..."

She pulled away. "Weird, because it sure looked like you," she said, her tone devoid of emotion. She shrugged, her expression unreadable. "Whatever. I don't own you, West. You can do what you want."

She turned on her heel, swiping a bottle of vodka from

the counter and ducking through the crowd.

"Monty!"

She didn't stop, didn't even falter.

"Dude..." Van said, shaking his head at me. "That was bad."

I ran my hands through my hair. "Come on, man, that wasn't on me. She cornered me while I was getting drinks for you idiots."

Davis stumbled over. "Wait, you didn't mean to kiss Tahlia?"

I shot him a dark look.

"Oh bro, you fucked up bad."

My jaw clenched. "I didn't ask Tahlia to kiss me, she just did it."

Davis and Van shared a glance.

"Yeah, chicks don't really care about the details," Davis said, pulling a face that said I'm screwed. "They definitely care when you lock lips with another girl though."

I blew out a long breath. How the fuck had this happened? Surely Monty had to know by now that I'd never kiss someone else. Not when we were together.

Or *pretending* to be together. I'd been forgetting that part a lot lately.

"Just leave it, let her calm down," Van said. "Annabelle and Harley will talk her down. She'll hear you out eventually."

I followed my best friend's advice, but it was easier said than done. I wanted to go to her and explain everything, but I knew he was right and so long as she was still steaming over what she'd seen she wouldn't want to hear it. I wandered into the living room at one point, searching the crowd for her without trying to look like I was doing it, but she was nowhere to be found.

* * *

It had been more than an hour and I hadn't laid eyes on her once.

I hated this feeling. Hated that there was tension between us. I could understand the hurt in her eyes when she'd caught me with Tahlia. But surely Monty knew the truth?

Tahlia meant nothing to me. Monty was the only one I cared about, and it had been that way for weeks now.

Pushing through the party, I stopped short when I entered the kitchen and found Monty poised to take a shot from the waistband of a truly wasted Davis.

"Woah there, killer," I said, sliding an arm around her waist and swinging her away from my teammate.

"Hey!" she cried, wriggling in my arms, but I held firm, carrying her towards the door.

"Let the girl take her shot, boyfriend buzzkill!" Davis called.

Ignoring his drunk ass, I put Monty on her feet and shepherded her out of the room. She swiped a half-empty bottle of tequila off the counter as she went, taking a deep swig and trying not to gag.

"Someone's in the mood to get ripped tonight," I said, wrapping my arms around her waist to steady her as she stumbled into the hall.

"Maybe shots just taste better when you do them out of a ball player's shorts," she said, her tone flat, making it clear she was mad at me.

"Trust me, you don't want to drink anything that's been warmed on Davis's balls."

She snorted a laugh, and I buried my face in her hair, running the tip of my nose over the length of her throat, relishing the feel of her in my arms. She shuddered at my touch, making me smile against her.

I loved the pliant way her body reacted to me, even when she was mad at me. Like she'd given up on some of the walls she'd been so adamant on putting up between us, and she couldn't help but respond to my touch.

"You want to do a shot out of anyone's shorts, make it mine," I murmured in her ear.

Turning in my arms, she scowled. "You were otherwise occupied."

She put her hands on her hips, daring me to deny it, and I raised my hands.

"It was against my will, I can promise you that. She didn't give me the chance to tell her I wasn't interested."

Monty rolled her eyes. "God, it must be so horrible being you."

A grin spread across my face at her blatant pouting, and I reached out to snake a hand over her hip, sliding it down to her perfect ass and tugging her closer. "Not when you're around." I brushed my mouth over the exposed skin below her ear, making her breath hitch. "I wanted it to be you."

She bit her bottom lip and the hand not clutching the bottle of tequila landed on my chest. She stared at it, slowly rubbing it up and down over my pec.

How much had she had to drink in the hour I'd left her alone?

"Ugh, why are you like this?" she demanded, but her tone had lost its stubborn edge, which meant she was close to forgiving me.

I smiled down at her. "Like what? Incredibly handsome, charming and an all-round great guy?"

"Exactly. It's so annoying."

She took another swig of the tequila, and I fought a

smile. She'd regret it tomorrow, but I knew better than to try to argue with her now.

She stared up at me through black lashes, slowly pressing up on her toes until our mouths were inches apart and my dick stirred in my jeans at the thought of those lips anywhere on me.

Her tongue poked out to lick her bottom lip and I swallowed hard.

"What are you doing?" I asked, my voice huskier than I expected.

A small smile spread across her face, her hand trailing down my chest and over my abs, pausing just above my waistband.

"Going back to the kitchen to take my shot out of Davis's pants." She pushed me away with a satisfied smile and made a beeline for the kitchen.

"Oh, no you don't!"

I snagged her wrist and tugged her back to me, taking the bottle of tequila from her. Squatting, I picked her up with one arm and slung her over my shoulder.

"What the hell are you doing?" she said, tugging at the back of my shirt.

"I told you, you want to do a shot out of anyone's waistband, make it mine."

I took the stairs two at a time, throwing open the door to my room, then kicking it shut behind us, before walking over and placing the bottle of tequila on the nightstand and dropping Monty on the bed.

She gave an indignant squeak as she bounced against the mattress.

"You can't be serious with this caveman routine."

"As a heart attack."

I swiped one of the shot glasses from my desk, then

stalked back to the nightstand to fill it with tequila. I stepped up to the side of the bed in front of Monty, slipping the glass into the waistband of my jeans.

She stared up at me, a mix of disbelief and anticipation in her eyes.

"Have at it, babe."

A sense of challenge filled her expression and she sat forward, shifting to the edge of the bed. My dick stirred. What I wouldn't give to feel Monty's perfect lips wrapped around my cock.

She leaned forward, her mouth opening to wrap around the shot glass. I stared down at her, so many X-rated thoughts about all the things I wanted to do with her running through my head.

Her warm tongue swept over my lower abs and she pulled the shot glass free with her teeth and suctioned her lips around the glass. She tilted her head back, the amber liquid sliding down her throat.

She pulled the glass from her lips with a look of triumph. "Your turn."

"Pour it out," I said, my voice husky, my eyes never leaving her.

She reached for the tequila, refilling the glass then getting to her feet. She lifted her black shirt, tucking it into the bottom of her bra and showing off the perfect curve of her hips and the smooth planes of her toned stomach.

Fuck, her body was pure fire. I wanted to run my mouth over every inch of her.

She tugged out the waistband of her mini skirt an inch and slid the glass in. Heat burned through me at the way she stared up at me, a seductive smile on her lips, my cock pressing against my zipper.

I never should have played this game. But the idea of

her incredible mouth anywhere near Davis's dick made me want to punch my teammate in the face.

Holding her by the hips, I bent down and pressed a kiss to the top of her torso, just below her bra. She sucked in a surprised breath, blowing it straight back out on a sigh, the sound spurring me on.

My mouth trailed down her stomach, tongue sweeping over her until I reached her waistband. I crouched low, hands wrapped around her hips to steady me, and glanced up at her.

She stared back with half hooded eyes, teeth biting her bottom lip.

Leaning in, I let my tongue brush over her skin, dipping as far beneath her waistband as I dared.

"West..." she breathed.

Pulling the shot glass from her waistband with my teeth, I stared up at her as I knocked it back, too distracted by the desire burning in her gaze to notice the burn of the liquor.

My thumbs brushed over her hip bones, hooking in her waistband. I dragged her skirt down an inch, my mouth closing over the exposed skin I'd just revealed.

She let out a soft noise and I did it again, my tongue sweeping over her soft skin.

Her fingers tangled in my hair. "West, please..."

I smiled against her. "What do you want, baby?"

My tongue trailed over her in wet, open-mouthed kisses.

"You," she said, breathless. "I want you."

I gripped the back of her bare thighs, still crouched beneath her. "You've had a lot to drink tonight. Are you sure this is what you want?"

The desire in her eyes morphed into disgruntled outrage in a matter of seconds.

"I know you're trying to be a gentleman right now and I

appreciate it, but I'm not so drunk that I'll regret this tomorrow. I don't want sweet West right now, I want the one who makes girls brag about the King of Campus giving them the best orgasm they've ever had."

I couldn't help my chuckle as I pushed to my feet, eyes locked with hers. "You sure?"

She smiled. "I'm so sure."

Sliding my fingers into her hair, I pulled her mouth to mine, my tongue sweeping into her mouth and making her moan against me.

"Jesus," she said when I guided her to the bed. "I could've come just from that kiss."

I chuckled, climbing on top of her. "Are you going to keep up a running commentary the whole time? Because I'm already under pressure with your demand for an orgasm worth bragging rights."

"I'll be quiet as a church mouse," she said, slapping a hand over her mouth and I dropped my head to her shoulder to stifle my laugh.

"Don't be silent." I ran my lips over her throat. "The noises you make when I touch you get me hard."

She nodded eagerly. "Got it. Orgasmic moans and words of encouragement only. No boner-killing commentary."

I couldn't help my smile as I lowered my mouth to hers, her lips parting eagerly. She was sweet and smart and so goddamn beautiful. We'd been leading up to this for months and now that I could finally have her, I never wanted to let her go.

We kissed until we were both grinding against each other, desperate for more.

When we broke apart, her cheeks were flushed with heat and her eyes heavy with lust. "Jesus, West."

"That's more like it."

I lifted her shirt and she reached up her arms so I could tug it over her head, my eyes roaming the soft flesh that spilled out of a black lace bra.

She reached back to unclip it, sliding the straps down her arms and flinging it across my room, leaving her bare from the waist up.

"Someone's keen," I said, lips gliding over the swell of her perfect tits.

"You have no idea how long I've wanted this."

I'd wanted this from the first time she'd kissed me and now that we were here, the moment was so much hotter than I'd ever imagined.

"About as much as I want it," I said, my mouth closing over her hardened nipple that was begging to be sucked.

Her back arched off the bed, her teeth sinking into her bottom lip as she moaned.

She looked incredible laid out on my bed, begging me to make her come. Monty had captivated me in a way no girl ever had, and I wanted nothing more than to make her moan my name.

As I worked my tongue over her other nipple, she arched into my mouth, her breath trembling along with the rest of her.

"Please, West..."

I smiled to myself as I kissed my way down her body.

She reached back to unzip her skirt and I slid it down her smooth legs, taking her panties too, leaving her bare on the bed in front of me.

"Fuck, Monty." I stroked myself through my jeans, my dick so hard I was in danger of blowing my load right now.

I ran a hand up the softness of her inner thigh, my mouth descending on her.

The first swipe of my tongue over her center had her hips bucking off the bed. The sweetest noises escaped her with every glide of my tongue, her fingers tangling in my hair as she rocked against my mouth. I slid a finger inside her, then added another, my tongue working in swirling strokes over her hot bud.

"Oh my god, West..."

Hearing her sigh in ecstasy just about tipped me over the edge and she hadn't even touched me.

I lapped at her until she trembled beneath me, her moans growing louder until her entire body tightened.

"Don't stop," she panted. "Please don't stop."

There was no way in hell I was going to stop when she was on the edge of coming against my tongue. Picking up the pace, I flicked my tongue over her in time with the fingers sliding in and out of her.

"Yes, West... oh my god..."

She threw her head back, crying out as her whole body arched off the bed, her hands gripping my head as she rode out her orgasm. I lapped at her until she fell back on the bed, fully satiated.

"Holy shit," she said, panting through her comedown.

I sat up, a satisfied grin on my face.

"That was so hot," she said on a deep sigh. "No one has ever made me come that hard."

I climbed onto the bed, lying beside her and tugging her into my arms. "I aim to please."

"We should probably do something about that," she said, motioning to the tent in my jeans.

I kissed the top of her head. "You don't have to."

She lifted her head, rolling across my chest to look at me. "What if I want to?"

The devilish glint in her eye was unmissable as she slowly unbuttoned my shirt.

"You don't know how long I've been waiting to get my tongue all over this body."

I chuckled, a look of awe crossing her face as she stared at my bare torso.

"How are you real?" she whispered.

Before I could answer her mouth descended, tongue swiping over the ridges of my abs. The feel of her warm mouth made me groan. I'd been picturing what her mouth would feel like on my cock for months and now she was running it all over me.

She unzipped my jeans, I lifted my hips so she could slide them down my legs, my hard cock springing free between us.

"Oh my god." She stared at it wide-eyed. "How the hell am I supposed to fit that in my mouth?"

I chuckled. "You don't have to if you don't want. You can just talk to him instead."

Reaching down, I stroked it a few times. She could blow on it at this point and the breeze would have me shooting off, that's how fucking turned on she made me.

"I'd rather introduce him to my tongue."

Before I could respond, her lips wrapped around the head, my cock disappearing inside her warm mouth as she swallowed me down.

"Fuck," I groaned, gripping the sheets in my fists.

Her mouth was so much better than anything I'd imagined. Warm and wet, she slid her tongue over every inch of me, pleasure shooting through me when I hit the back of her throat.

"Fuck!"

I reached down to brush her hair out of her eyes.

"That feels so damn good, baby."

She smiled up at me and the sight had me ready to shoot.

"I'm not going to last long, not with your mouth wrapped around me like that."

She sucked harder, tongue swirling around the tip before gliding me into her mouth until I hit the back of her throat again. I groaned loud enough for the whole house to hear even over the music, my orgasm building at the base of my spine, legs tensing.

Monty reached between us, her fingers closing over my balls and tugging, making my hips shoot off the bed.

"Fuck, babe." I threaded my fingers through her hair, my hips thrusting into her mouth. "I'm going to come."

I expected her to pull away and jerk me until I came, but her mouth stayed put, lips moving up and down as she sucked harder.

"Shit, Monty. I'm going to fucking come, baby."

She glanced up, her eyes locking with mine and she moaned long and loud with my dick still in her mouth; it was enough to put a porn star to shame. The vibration combined with her phenomenal tongue was enough to send me over the edge, white hot pleasure tearing through me. I spilled into the back of her throat, but she didn't hesitate, swallowing it down, tongue gliding over my shaft until I was fully spent.

I fell back on the bed, throwing an arm over my eyes. "Holy shit, babe. That was the best blow job I've ever had."

She crawled up my body, settling herself against me and I lifted my arm to wrap it around her.

She smiled up at me.

"I aim to please," she said with smug satisfaction.

Chapter Nineteen

MONTY

I woke in West's bed, his warm body wrapped around me from behind, his morning wood poking me in the ass, and a pounding on the door.

"Yo, West, man. You got a visitor," Jericho called through the door.

"Tell them to fuck off, I'm busy," West called back.

His arms tightened around my waist, and he buried his face in my neck.

"Er... I'm not going to tell your mom that, man."

My eyes shot open at the same time West's hands slid from my body.

"My mom's here?" He ran a hand through his hair, moving from the bed to grab a fresh pair of sweats and a t-shirt from his closest.

I clutched the sheet to my naked body. "Should I..."

Smiling, he leaned across the bed to press a quick kiss to mouth.

"You can get dressed and come meet my mom. Or you can stay here and hide out. Totally up to you, babe."

Those blue eyes stared back at me. Patient. Encouraging. Everything he'd been the whole time we were together. Not only had Mr. Anti-Commitment proven he could be the best fake boyfriend, but he'd given me one hell of an orgasm last night too.

I had a pounding headache this morning thanks to the tequila, but last night had still been damn near perfect.

We'd crossed every boundary and broken every rule. We'd fallen asleep in each other's arms and I'd drifted off, finally letting my walls down and admitting to myself how hard I'd fallen for him. I'd spent the past few months trying to deny that my feelings had strayed from fake to genuine. But there was no denying it in the sober light of day.

The jealousy that had burned in my chest watching Tahlia kiss him last night had made it painfully clear.

I wanted West to be mine and not in a fake way.

"I better go see what my mom is doing here." He kissed me again and made a beeline for the door, closing it behind him.

Throwing off the sheets, I stepped into my skirt and pulled my shirt over my head. If last night's party outfit didn't spell walk-of-shame... but going downstairs to meet West's mom in one of his t-shirts and a pair of his sweats would be worse. I brushed my teeth with the spare toothbrush he'd taken to keeping here for me and sprayed myself with his cologne. I smelled like West, and I didn't hate it one bit.

Slipping from his room, I padded down the stairs quietly, most of the guys still asleep after last night's rager. I hoped West's mom wasn't anti-parties, because it was clear from the mess spread across just about every inch of the house that one had gone off here last night.

I stopped in the hall outside the living room and West's voice floated through the doorway.

"What are you doing here, Mom?" His tone wasn't exactly brimming with warmth for the woman who'd birthed him.

"Can't I stop by to visit my baby boy?" Her voice was teasing and light.

"You can come see me whenever you want, you know that. But a text or phone call would have been nice. We had kind of a big night."

His mom laughed. "It's nothing I haven't seen before, sweetheart. I was young once too."

West sighed.

"My, my. Someone is crabby this morning. You really don't want your mother here right now, do you?"

There was a pause in their conversation, and I debated whether to use it to walk in and introduce myself.

"Have you got a girl here? Is that the problem?"

West didn't respond.

"You do have a girl in your room. Can I meet her?"

"Yeah, you can meet her."

Another silence.

"You've never introduced me to a girl before. Does that mean this one's special?"

I bit my lip, fighting my smile as I waited for West's response.

"No, Mom. There's nothing special between us, we're just friends."

My stomach dropped. And I gripped the wall to steady me.

Just friends?

No friend of mine had ever gone down on me the way West had last night. Or spent the past few months texting me to see how my day was. Or kissing me at basketball games in front of the entire student body.

The truth hit me like a Mack truck to the chest. I'd been kidding myself into thinking any of that meant anything at all to West. I'd thought somewhere in the middle of our fake relationship that we'd been building something real.

But for him it had all been fake.

The hurt slicing through me threatened to break me, my eyes pricking with tears. I couldn't deal with this when my defenses were already brutalized this morning by my hangover.

West had made his intentions clear from the start. He didn't do relationships or commitment. All he cared about was making it to the NBA and having fun along the way, which meant while I'd been falling for West these past few months, he'd been quietly keeping me at a distance.

All the compliments, the sweet words, the protective gestures. Had it really just been a play to get me into bed?

"Oh honey, I know how important basketball is to you and I respect that. But there's more to life than the game. When are you going to get serious about someone?"

West let out an exasperated sigh. "I don't know, Mom, but it's not today, okay?"

"Why not? Is she not special enough?"

My stomach tightened and I waited for the painful blow I knew was coming.

"Nothing is more important to me than basketball and making it to the NBA. You know that."

I flinched, my heart shattering in my chest.

Only none of this was a surprise. West had never tried

to hide his single-minded focus on basketball; I'd just managed to convince myself that I was different.

But I was a fool. Just another in a long string of idiotic girls who'd fallen for a fuckboy. I'd broken my own rules and ended up exactly where I'd expected to.

I had no one to blame but myself.

"Honey..." West's mom started, but he cut her off.

"Did you come here to lecture me, or do you want to spend some time together? Give me fifteen minutes to shower and we'll go to breakfast."

Only minutes ago, I'd been lauding him in my head as a near-perfect guy. Now I wanted to puke in his sock drawer and delete his number from my phone.

I bolted up the stairs, shutting the door as quietly as I could manage, searching his room for my shoes. Finding my phone on the nightstand, I clicked the screen, sinking onto the bed to stare at the string of text messages from Alec, my eyes barely seeing the words.

He'd been texting me last night during the party and had clearly started again as soon as he'd woken.

> *Please meet me on campus today. I just want to talk, Monty. That's all x*

"Babe?" West said, somehow standing in front of me. "Didn't feel like meeting my mom, huh?"

I stared back at the boy who had unknowingly torn my heart out. Even looking at him hurt.

There's nothing between us, we're just friends.

Nothing is more important to me than basketball.

"Hey, you okay?" West asked, crouching in front of me.

I nodded, forcing a smile on my face. "Yeah, just battling a hangover."

He grinned back at me. "Downing tequila straight from the bottle will do that to you."

So will falling for a fuckboy you knew wanted nothing more than sex.

West disappeared into the bathroom, coming back with a glass of water and extra-strength painkillers. "These will make you feel better. Want me to make you some food?"

I shook my head, knocking back the water and pills without a word.

He eyed me carefully. "You sure you're okay?"

"Yeah, of course."

Leaning down, he pressed a kiss to the top of my head, and I fought back the tears that burned the back of my eyes, avoiding his gaze.

"I'm going to take a shower. You want to come grab breakfast with me and my mom?"

I shook my head, my mind searching for an excuse. "I can't. I need to stop by my professor's office to get her notes on my submission, And, um... then I have to hit the library to work on her edits. Thanks though, you have fun with your mom."

He nodded, heading for the bathroom. "It won't be as much fun without you there, babe."

He winked at me, then shut the bathroom door, the shower turning on a few seconds later.

Did he lie like that to every girl, or was I just extra special?

Bitterness washed over me. I'd kidded myself into believing I could survive the bed-hopping Pierson basketball star. And I'd been so wrong.

Overcome with the urge to get the hell out of here, I

shoved my feet into my shoes and grabbed my phone, replying to Alec.

I'll meet you, but it has to be now.

Nothing could hurt me anymore than I was already. May as well let life pummel me with everything it was intent on throwing at me.

I'd gotten caught up with West in the first place because of Alec.

And I just wanted this entire mess to be over.

* * *

Fifteen minutes later I was seated across from Alec at a table in the back of the campus coffee house.

He'd ordered me a double-shot latte, both our drinks sitting between us on the table, along with a slice of coffee cake, my favorite.

Some of the boys at the basketball house had thankfully woken and entertained West's mom in the kitchen, which meant I'd been able to sneak out of the house in the worst and only walk of shame I'd ever made.

Meeting my stalker ex wasn't exactly my first choice of activity after having the guy I was falling for rip my heart out. But I was tired, hungover and emotionally wrung out. I wanted to get this over with and I was still clinging to the desperate hope that if I took the time to spell out to Alec yet again that I had no intention of getting back with him that he might finally accept it and move on.

Maybe I was naïve. In fact, I knew I was. But part of me still wanted this to end amicably, given we were from the same town and had cared about each other once.

If Alec was no longer a problem, that meant there was no need for West and I to keep up the pretense of a fake relationship. I'd be free from both of them to move on with my life.

"You said you wanted to talk?" I stared blankly at Alec, fighting the pounding in my head and the swirling in my stomach. My mind was still numb, West's words to his mom playing over and over in my head like a bad pop song I couldn't shake.

'When are you going to get serious about someone?'

'I don't know, Mom, but it's not today.'

My stomach rolled, my chest splitting in two all over again at the reminder.

"Are you okay?" Alec frowned at me. "Tough morning?"

I snorted. "You could say that, I guess."

It certainly wasn't one of my best. I'd woken on such a high after West and I finally crossed the line last night, only to come crashing back down. I was a damn fool for ignoring my own advice and better judgment. I'd known West would only lead to heartbreak and here I was, disgustingly hungover, about to break down over our fake relationship in front of my ex-boyfriend.

"I'm here for you, Monty. Whatever you need, I'm always happy to help."

I sighed. "Alec, what I need from you is to leave me alone and move on. Please tell me you understand that."

His eyes tightened at the corners. "I don't understand it. Why would you push me away like this? You need me, Monty."

Frustration flooded me. What I needed was a bacon and egg sandwich, a hot shower and a long, hard cry on Imogen and Stella's shoulders.

I didn't know what else to say to Alec, what else to do, to make him see that I didn't want to be with him. I'd faked a relationship with the King of Campus to escape him.

"I'm pushing you away because it's over between us. It's been over for a long time."

Alec stared at the table. "It's because of the basketball player."

My grip tightened on my cup. "It's got nothing to do with him."

Not anymore.

When I'd woken up this morning I'd been so sure about telling West how I felt. Now I knew I had to end it with him. Only how could I when Alec was still as persistent as ever? If I broke up with my fake boyfriend, Alec's attempts to win me back would only escalate.

I was stuck in a mess of my own making unless I could convince Alec to finally move on.

"I don't understand what you want with me, Alec. There are plenty of other girls out there."

He shook his head, reaching out to take my hand where it sat on the table between us, but I pulled away. "None of them are you. You're not like other girls, Monty."

I resisted the urge to roll my eyes. "I'm *exactly* like other girls."

Alec's gaze locked with mine, a strange edge to his voice. "Not to me. To me, you're everything."

Chapter Twenty

WEST

I halted inside the door of the coffee house, the freshman girl who'd been behind me bumping into me, her eyes widening when she saw who I was, apologizing profusely. I shot her a quick smile, my focus returning to Monty.

She sat at a table in the far corner. And Alec was across from her.

She'd told me she couldn't come to breakfast with my mom because she was going to her professor's office then was headed to the library to study.

My mom and I had decided to cook at the house with the guys, so I'd wrapped things up fast and stopped by the coffee house to grab some drinks before dropping by the library to see Monty.

But she was here with him... *What the hell was going on?*

I threaded through the scattered tables, barely acknowledging the people who called my name to congratulate me on the team's recent win.

I came to a stop at their table, and Monty's eyes widened. "West, hi."

Two half-empty cups and a piece of cake sat between them on the table.

So, they'd been here a while then.

"You remember Alec," Monty said, shifting uncomfortably in her seat.

The guy stared daggers at me.

"How could I forget," I said, returning the favor.

Monty had been acting weird when I'd come back to my room this morning, but I'd assumed it was a combination of her hangover and the surprise visit from my mom. Or maybe it was all the lines we'd crossed together last night.

I'd suspected Alec had been the one texting her at the party, but why the fuck would she agree to meet with him? And why hadn't she told me?

An awkward silence fell, and my eyes snagged on the essay on the table.

"Did you get your submission back from your professor?" I asked, picking it up and frowning at the name across the top.

Emily Montgomery.

"Who's Emily?"

Alec scoffed and a hint of pink colored Monty's cheeks.

"He doesn't even know your real name and I'm supposed to believe he cares about you?" Alec said as though I wasn't standing right beside him. "All he cares about is free throws and getting laid."

Emily Montgomery.

Monty.

Fuck, how had I never put that together?

"That's not..." Monty trailed off, shaking her head and looking like she'd rather be anywhere but here right now. The worst part was, I couldn't tell if it was my surprise appearance that was making her feel that way or her stalker ex.

Anger boiled in my chest that she was even here. Alec had terrified her for weeks, now he sat across from her like her fucking savior in the face of the big bad basketball player?

"You don't know a fucking thing about me, man." I narrowed my eyes on the weasel. "But I know all about you—"

"I think it's time to go," Monty said, pushing to her feet, shoving her submission in her backpack and grabbing her coat. "Thanks for the coffee, Alec, but I meant what I said. Today and every other day."

She didn't even spare me a glance before brushing past me and heading for the door. I followed, the icy wind hitting my face as she stopped on the path outside.

"Care to tell me why you were having coffee with that asshole?" I asked, shoving my hands in the pockets of my jacket to rein in my temper.

She wasn't my real girlfriend. And even if she were, I had no right to tell her who she could have coffee with. But I'd be lying if I said walking in to find her with him didn't tear me up inside. The guy was a creep, and I couldn't understand what it was going to take for her to finally cut him off. Monty was compassionate and it was an admirable quality, but some people didn't deserve her compassion. Alec had surpassed that point months, maybe even a year ago.

"He messaged me this morning and asked me to meet him. He said he just wanted to talk."

She looked down at her shoes, at the students coming and going from the coffee house, at the garden along the walkway. Anywhere but at me.

"Hey," I said, taking her hand and closing the space between us. "What's going on with you? Talk to me."

She finally looked at me, a smile that didn't come close to reaching her eyes plastered on her face.

"Nothing, I'm fine." She shrugged. "Just feeling weird after meeting with Alec."

I studied her, some emotion I couldn't name hiding behind her eyes. Something was definitely up, but if she didn't want to tell me I couldn't force her.

I brushed my thumb lightly over her knuckles. "You know if there's something going on with you, you can talk to me. We're friends first."

Even as the words left my mouth, they sounded like a lie.

Just like they'd been a lie when I'd said them to my mom this morning. But Mom was the last person I wanted to confide in, especially about finally finding someone I wanted to commit to.

Fuck being friends, I was so past that now. Monty was more than that.

I'd gone into this thinking we'd have some fun together, maybe help each other out and get each other off, then go our separate ways. But now I hated the thought of being without her, of not being able to text her about our days or watch her school my teammates about their extracurricular habits. Somehow, she'd become so embedded in my life, the thought of her not being there made me sweat like a co-dependent fool.

Faking it had been fun, but the idea of a real relationship didn't have me running the same way it would have months ago. All because of Monty. She'd helped me realize that not all relationships had to be as screwed up as my parents'.

I wanted this to be real with her. And I wanted it to be genuine.

I wanted her.

"Listen, Monty..." I said, lifting a hand to tuck her hair behind her ear.

She stiffened and pulled back.

"I have to go," she said, avoiding my eye again. "I said I'd meet Stella at the studio to help her with an art project."

I frowned. "Okay..."

She glanced at me quickly before looking away. "I'll see you later, okay?"

"Sure."

Then she disappeared down the walkway, leaving me as confused as I'd been that first day on the quad.

Chapter Twenty-One

MONTY

Things had been strained between me and West for the past few weeks, since the visit from his mom and the coffee house with Alec.

He'd left for winter break four days later and I'd managed to avoid him before he went, making excuses about assignments and getting my coursework done so I could celebrate the holidays with my friends.

We'd been messaging over the break, but I'd made the same excuses to avoid him since he'd been back when he asked about grabbing dinner together after practice or me staying over at the basketball house. I'd even been avoiding the library in case he showed up with coffee.

I knew I was being weak and borderline cruel and I should just end it with him, but I didn't have the strength to do it.

Just like every other time I'd talked to him, Alec had ignored my request to move on and leave me alone. I'd spent more than an hour crying to Imogen and Stella about West before the break, only to open the door to our suite on Christmas Day to find a giant bouquet of lilies and a card from Alec that said he was thinking of me.

Alec thinking of me was the exact opposite of what I wanted.

And me constantly thinking about West wasn't what I wanted either.

But after West's public display at the Kensington game and how loved up we'd been around campus and at the party at the basketball house—when that girl hadn't been trying to shove her tongue down his throat—people were starting to talk.

And not all of it was good.

"I heard she jumped him in the quad against his will and that's how they met. Talk about eager to bag a ball player," a stunning brunette with insanely long legs and curvy waist said to her friend as they passed our booth by the front window of Ruby's. It was the only decent restaurant within walking distance from campus, which meant it was impossible to avoid the basketball crowd.

"That's not how it happened!" Imogen called after them, and I wanted to sink down in my seat.

"Imogen, that's pretty much exactly how it had happened," I hissed.

She shot me a look. "Those thirsty bitches don't need to know that."

Stella gave my hand an encouraging squeeze. "Nobody talks smack about you on our watch."

The two girls stopped, glancing back at Imogen. "Excuse me?"

"I said, that's not what happened between West and Monty."

They sauntered back to the table.

"Oh my god, you're her," the brunette said, eyes scanning me.

"It's not some fling," Stella cut in. "They're dating."

A pitying smile crossed the girl's face, and she crossed her arms over her chest. "Dating doesn't mean a thing to West or any of those guys. You might be dating today, but it doesn't mean you'll still be dating tomorrow. Or that you're special."

"Thanks for the tip," I said, staring blankly back at her. Her words had hit exactly where she'd wanted them too, but I wouldn't let her see it.

I'd learned all too well exactly the kind of actor West Wright was. I didn't need her spelling it out for me. My shattered heart was proof enough.

She stared down her nose at me. "He'll be onto someone else by next week."

Imogen smiled sweetly at her. "While you'll still be begging for one of them to look your way."

The girl stared daggers at Imogen, just as the bell over the door jangled and a loud group of guys entered the restaurant clad in navy and white.

The brunette's face split into a grin.

"Here's your boy now," she said with smug satisfaction. "Would be a shame if someone were to steal him right out from under you."

I lifted a shoulder as if her threats had no effect on me. "Do your worst, hon."

She sauntered in the direction of the players, who'd stopped by the counter to talk to some of the football guys, her ass swaying in her tiny skirt.

I knew I had to break up with West, but baiting another

girl into tempting him and doing it for me was a brutal way to go about it. For the both of us.

Yet a small part of me—the part that clearly lacked any kind of self-preservation or respect for my shattered heart—couldn't stomach the idea of West taking the bait.

"Relax," Imogen said, misreading my discomfort. "Despite what he said to his mom, I think you can trust him."

Even though I'd tried to shut down my feelings, watching West flirt with another girl wasn't high on my priority list of things I wanted to do today.

That didn't mean I could tear my eyes away from the brunette as she reached him, a broad smile stretched across his perfect face. She brushed a hand along his arm and when he glanced down at her she pushed up on her toes, clinging to his shoulder and whispering in his ear.

"I wonder what desperate proposition she's making," Stella said.

My stomach tightened. He was listening to whatever it was. He hadn't immediately brushed her off like I'd been secretly hoping for. But what did I expect? Our relationship wasn't real. Especially not for him. And I'd spent the last few weeks avoiding him. He couldn't think we were doing well.

"He's not even listening to her," Imogen said, giving me her best I-told-you-so look.

Watching West talk to a girl who so overtly wanted him was like picking at an already bleeding wound. I wanted him to want me the same way I wanted him. Only I couldn't let it show. And wanting something wouldn't make it true.

"My god, you're still so into him," Imogen said, scanning my face.

I bit my lip, tears pricking the backs of my eyes, but I refused to let them fall.

Resigned, I nodded, and Imogen's eyes filled with worry, both of us glancing back to West and his friends. He was still leaning down to hear the brunette, scanning the restaurant over her shoulder as though he wasn't really listening.

Then his gaze landed on me. And his face split into a ruinous smile.

Damn it. Why did he have to look at me that way?

I was so screwed. Staying away from him these past two weeks meant I'd been able to fool myself into believing I could get over him. That he was just some stupid fake boyfriend plan gone wrong. But he was so far under my skin, I had no idea how to dig him out.

He muttered something to the brunette and walked away, leaving her staring after him in disbelief.

He made his way over to our table and slid into the booth beside me.

"Hey, babe."

Sliding an arm around my shoulders, he smiled down at me like he was genuinely happy to see me.

I glanced up at him, Imogen's assessing eyes burning against my skin. "Hey."

He pressed a kiss to my temple. "Missed you."

It was like he knew exactly the right things to say to make me break inside. I pressed my lips together, trying to fend off the emotion threatening to overwhelm me.

Why did he have to be this sweet? If it wasn't real for him, why bother?

I glanced at him again, those blue eyes watching me.

Why does he have to look at me like that?

Why does he have to touch me the way he does?

Why did he have to rebuff that brunette the moment he spotted me?

My fragile heart couldn't take it. And I was tired of fighting it.

"I've missed you too," I said quietly, the truth out there before I could stop it.

The smile that spread across his face was enough to ruin me all over again.

"Did you miss me too, Monty?" Bant said, sliding into the booth.

Imogen's gaze slid to Bant. "When would she have had time to miss you? You're always around."

Stella shot me a look. Imogen was always frank, whatever she was thinking usually coming straight out of her mouth without a second thought. But she was also an insane flirt, charming every guy with a bat of her lashes. Her increasing disdain for Bant only meant one thing... Imogen was into him. And she was hating every second of it.

"You're one to talk, sweetheart," Bant said, undeterred by her snark. "You're not exactly MIA from most of these social outings either."

He tried to steal a fry from her plate, and she slapped his hand away.

"Come on, I'm hungry. Fending off thirsty women is hard work, you know."

Imogen rolled her eyes, muttering something that sounded like "poor basketball baby".

Van slid into the booth next to Bant, and Stella shifted in her seat beside me.

I shot her a quizzical look but she just smiled, sliding her plate in Bant's direction to offer her fries.

"You idiots leave me with the basketball bunnies again

and I'm going to dip your toothbrushes in the toilet bowl," Van said to his teammates.

West ignored him. "Sorry to crash your dinner," he said quietly to me.

I shrugged, trying to pretend like everything he did, everywhere he was touching me, wasn't lighting me up inside. "It's fine."

He reached out, hooking a finger under my chin and tilted my face to his. "I meant it when I said I missed you."

I bit my lip. "I meant it too."

"You've been avoiding me." His eyes narrowed on mine, searching for answers.

I could have sworn that was genuine affection in his eyes, but I had to stop fooling myself. I knew the truth, I'd heard it directly from his own mouth.

"I've just been busy." The lie fell from my lips so easily.

He nodded, those bright blue eyes studying me. "Come home with me tonight? There's something I need to talk to you about." He glanced at our friends. "Alone."

I started to make excuses and his hand brushed my cheek.

"Please Monty. It's important."

Before I'd even registered what I was doing, I nodded, and West closed the space between us, his mouth edging towards mine.

"Don't even think about making out with her, man," Van said, saving me from myself.

We both looked up, heat coloring my cheeks.

"I swear to God, you two wait until I'm around to start fooling around. Is getting it on in public your kink?"

"Try sharing a wall with West," Bant said, tossing one of Stella's fries in the air and catching it in his mouth. "They weren't exactly quiet when they got it on at the party."

I covered my face with my hands, embarrassment flooding me. There was no way I could have stayed quiet while West was giving me one of the best orgasms of my life. Too bad I'd thought we'd been solidifying our connection that night, while West had just been waiting to score.

"Shut the fuck up, man," West said, throwing a fry at Bant across the table.

He caught it against his chest and tossed it in his mouth, chewing it with a shit-eating grin.

The bell over the door jangled and I glanced behind Bant, my gaze landing on Alec coming through the door with two friends I'd never seen before. The guy was tall and lanky with curly black hair, the girl cute with a short, light brown bob and wide smile.

Alec glanced over at our booth, and I stiffened. West followed my gaze, his arm tightening around my shoulders.

Alec's eyes never left me as he slid into one of the booths along the front window at the other end of the restaurant.

"You know what, I'm going over there," West said.

I blanched. "To do what?"

"Tell him to get the fuck over it."

"Who we fucking up?" Van asked at the bite in West's tone, turning in his seat to scan the dinner.

"The creepy ex," Bant said, doing the same.

Imogen pulled a face. "Alec's here? Screw going over there to talk, I'm going to go over there and beat his ass."

West grunted in agreement. "I like that plan even better."

"Nobody is doing anything if it's not what Monty wants," Stella said, and I gave her hand a grateful squeeze under the table.

"He's not even doing anything. Let's just leave him alone," I said, hoping they'd all drop it.

"I don't like the way he looks at you," West said, his eyes still on Alec across the room.

"You don't need to do this," I said, trying to draw his attention back to me.

It worked, his head snapping in my direction. "The guy threw a rock through your window."

"We don't know that for sure."

Imogen rolled her eyes. "The only person who believes that is you, Monts. Let West go caveman on his ass and maybe he'll finally get the message."

Me telling Alec to move on hadn't worked, so maybe sending West over there to talk to him wouldn't be such a bad thing.

"Fine," I said. "But no threats."

"We can't promise that, Monts," Van said, sliding out of the booth, Bant following.

"Wait, you're all going?" I asked, eyes wide with alarm.

"We're a team, a trio, a gang," Bant said with a wink.

"You're pack of fools, is what you are," Imogen said.

He blew her a kiss and followed West and Van, West striding across the restaurant like he was ready to deliver a beatdown.

"Ugh, I feel sick," I said, dropping my eyes to the table.

Only I couldn't keep them there.

West stopped next to the booth, towering over everyone at the table. Van stood beside him looking more imposing than I'd ever seen him. Bant, on the other hand, slouched on one of the stools at the counter, elbows resting on it like he didn't have a care in the world. He winked at a leggy waitress who walked by, making her smile.

West leaned down, placing one hand on the back of the

booth behind Alec's head, the other on the table as he spoke.

Alec said something back, and Van piped up.

"I wish we could hear them," Stella said, eyes glued across the room.

I bit the inside of my cheek. "Me too."

West stood tall, saying one last thing to Alec before striding back across the restaurant with his teammates in tow.

"So... how did it go?" Imogen sing-songed.

West shrugged, sliding into the seat next to me and putting an arm around my shoulders again.

I glanced at Van and Bant, who stared back at me, expressions giving nothing away.

"That's it? A shrug? You're really not going to tell us what you said?"

West shifted in his seat. "I just told the guy that your time together was finished, you're with me now. And if he keeps harassing you, he'll have the whole basketball team gunning for him."

"Why would the rest of the basketball team care about my ex-boyfriend?"

"They don't," Bant said, stealing a fry from Imogen's plate and earning himself another slap. "They care about West, which means they care about you."

"We're a family, Monty," Van added. "And you're a part of that."

My chest twisted with anguish. God, heartbreak sucked.

"Oh shit, is she going to bawl? I'm no good with crying women," Bant said, looking alarmed.

Imogen rolled her eyes. "Absolutely no one is surprised that you're no good with women."

"You okay?" West asked, squeezing my shoulders.

I looked up at him and at least eight different emotions swelled in my chest.

How had kissing him in the quad been both the best and worst decision I'd ever made?

Chapter Twenty-Two

WEST

"What did you say to Alec tonight?" Monty asked, dropping her purse on the desk in my room.

I hadn't been imagining it. Things had been weird between us before I'd left for winter break, and they were still weird since I'd come back to campus. She'd been avoiding me, dodging my calls, sending short replies to my texts.

She was pulling away from me, and I had no idea why.

There was no denying what I'd felt when I'd seen her across the restaurant tonight. A hot brunette had been whispering in my ear about all the ways she wanted to ride my dick and I couldn't have cared less. The only thing I'd cared about was seeing Monty. And working out whatever weird tension was hanging between us. I still didn't understand why she'd gone to see Alec or why she'd lied to me about it. And why she'd been pulling away from me every day since.

I couldn't shake the feeling it had something to do with us hooking up at the party. Did she regret that we'd crossed the line?

"I told Alec the truth," I said, tossing my jacket on the back of my chair. "That you and I are together, so you and him were done. And it's time he moved on and left you the hell alone."

She glanced at the floor, biting the inside of her cheek. "But that's not true."

I stilled. "Which part?"

She wasn't seriously thinking about getting back with him, was she?

"The main part, the part we've been faking all along. We're not together."

My chest tightened. She was going to call it all off and tell me our fake relationship was over.

Only this wasn't fake for me anymore, and I didn't want to lose her.

I'd tried to tell her outside the coffee house before the holidays, but she'd pulled away from me. I didn't want this distance between us, I wanted to be close to her again, to tuck her under my arm and show everyone that we were together.

I'd never felt that way before. And I'd spent the past two weeks trying to find the right time to tell her. Sinking the winning basket during a game in front of a packed house was nothing compared to how it felt knowing I wanted take my shot with a girl who had totally consumed me.

I took a deep breath. "Maybe we should be together."

Her gaze connected with mine, her expression pained. "Don't do that."

"Do what? Tell you I want to be with you?"

She shook her head. "Don't say things you don't mean."

I narrowed my eyes at her. "Who says I don't mean it?"

She turned away from me, shaking her head. "I can't do this."

I crossed the room, taking her elbow and turning her to face me. "You can't do what? I'm telling you I want to be with you, and I mean it. These past few months together have been some of the best I've had. You've come to mean everything to me, Monty."

When she looked at me her eyes were filled with tears, and I wanted to pull her into my arms, only I knew she'd push me away.

"I heard you," she said, her voice so small it made my stomach twist. "I heard you with your mom the morning after the party. You told her we were just friends, that I was nothing special and that basketball was the only thing you cared about."

My stomach bottomed out. *She'd heard that?*

That was why she'd been pulling away from me. She'd heard me lie to my mom and believed every word as truth.

"Fuck." I ran my hands through my hair, thinking back over the conversation that day.

"There's no point in faking this anymore," she said.

The hurt in her eyes made my heart seize in my chest. I hated that I was the one who'd made her feel that way.

"Monty, I didn't mean any of it, I can promise you that. I only said we were friends to get my mom off my back."

She shook her head. "You told me from the start you don't do relationships. I should have listened..." She tugged free and sat on the bed, looking utterly defeated.

I followed, crouching in front of her, desperate to make her understand.

She was slipping through my fingers, but I didn't want her to throw in the towel and walk away from this.

"My parents have a terrible relationship. They both sleep with other people. I've never had a good example of a committed relationship, so it's never been something that was a priority for me." I took her hand again. "Until you, Monty."

She stared back at me, confusion clear on her face.

"I don't confide in my mom. All that stuff about us being friends and me being focused on basketball... I said it so she'd stop asking questions. That's all. I want to be with you, I've wanted it for weeks. I just had no fucking idea how to tell you because I had no idea if you felt the same way. You were all about boundaries and rules and walls between us, I had no idea if you felt anything for me."

Her brow pinched. "I wanted boundaries because I knew how easy it would be for my feelings to become real. I was scared it was going to happen, and I'd be left heartbroken when you didn't feel the same way." A tear slid down her cheek. "And it's exactly what happened."

I dropped to my knees, sliding in closer. "Your feelings for me are real?"

She stared down at her hands, nodding.

"Then it's not what happened," I said, swallowing hard. "Because my feelings for you are real too. And for the first time in as long as I can remember, I want a relationship. I want everything with you."

I cupped her face, tilting her head up and wiping her tears.

"I want us."

She gave me a watery smile. "So, all this time I've been trying to figure out the most painless way to end it between us, and you've been trying to figure out how to tell me you want me?"

I laughed. "We're off to a great start."

Sitting beside her, I cupped her cheek, fingers brushing over her soft skin.

"Please believe me when I say I want this. With the exception of letting Tahlia get the jump on me, I think I've been a pretty good fake boyfriend."

The smallest smile crossed her face. "You've been the best fake boyfriend."

"So, then we know I can do it. I want you, Monty. Only you, nobody else."

She wiped at her tears. "I want you too."

Hope unfurled in my chest at the thought I might be getting this girl for real.

"So, we're doing this?"

She smiled back. "Yeah, we're doing this."

I pulled her into my arms and rolled on top of her, her tears turning to laughter.

"What the hell are you doing?"

"My first job as boyfriend is going to be to make you come so hard the whole basketball house knows you're mine."

Her eyes widened. "That's definitely the kind of relationship goal I can get onboard with."

My mouth dropped to hers, my hand coming to caress her cheek. Her lips parted, her tongue brushing mine in slow, meaningful strokes.

I cared about this girl, and I wanted to give this a real shot.

Pulling away, she gently pushed me off her and got to her feet. She shoved me back onto my elbows on the bed.

"I want to play too," she said, pulling her top over her

head to reveal a purple lace bra. I hope I got to see every single piece of lace in her collection on my bedroom floor at some point. This girl in lingerie was a goddamn wet dream.

She gripped the bottom of my t-shirt and tugged it over my head, her tongue absently running over her bottom lip at the sight of my abs, as she moved south to my sweats, sliding them down my legs.

"That's quite a view," she said, eyes heavy with lust.

"It's yours whenever you want it. And you can do more than look at it."

A smile split her beautiful face and I wanted to grip her waist and pull her down on top of me. But she wanted to take charge, so I was going to let her.

She unzipped her skirt, letting it drop to the floor, revealing a matching thong. She reached back to unclip her bra, her movements torturously slow as she slid it down her arms and tossed it aside.

I swallowed hard, my dick tenting in my boxers and I slid them off with the eagerness of a sixteen-year-old boy about to get laid for the first time. But this was a first for me. It was the first time in a long time—maybe ever—that I was going to sleep with someone I genuinely cared about. That I wanted to wake up to the next day and fuck all over again.

Monty was everything to me, and I wanted everything with her.

"You okay over there?" she asked with a small smile.

I nodded, not taking my eyes off her amazing rack.

Fuck, I wanted to touch her so badly. My fingers itched to caress her smooth skin and feel her against me, but I kept my hands fisted at my sides.

She hooked her thumbs in the waistband of her panties, gliding them down her legs.

Then she was naked in front of me.

"Fuck, Monty..." I choked out.

She didn't wait for me to put my tongue back in my mouth, closing the space between us and gripping my shoulders to steady herself as she climbed into my lap. My hands closed around her waist, one sliding over her round ass, and she rocked her hips against my steeled shaft.

Her teeth sunk into her bottom lip, her eyes turning glassy. "Oh, that feels so good."

I slipped a hand between us, thumbing her clit while she moved and making her gasp.

"Oh my God, West..."

"Yeah, baby?"

"That feels so good. I want you inside me."

I dropped my mouth to her throat, sucking on her skin and moving along her collarbone. "Not yet. I want you nice and wet for me."

She groaned and started to grind faster.

"So needy..." I teased. "We're not in a rush. We can take all night."

I knew the words were a lie the second I uttered them. I wanted to be inside her just as badly as she wanted me there.

She ran a hand over my hair, pulling my head back so I was looking her in the eye.

"I've never wanted someone inside me as much as I want you right now."

To prove her point, she slammed her mouth against mine, our tongues tangling in a hot, open-mouthed kiss that reminded me what it felt like to have her mouth wrapped around my dick.

Fuck anymore foreplay. She wanted this and so did I.

Snaking one arm around her waist to keep her steady, I leaned over to grab a condom from the nightstand.

"You sure you want to do this right now?" I asked, her eyes trained on my package as I slid the condom on.

"Shut up and fuck me."

A grin spread across my face as she gripped my shoulders again and straddled me once more. I guided my cock to her entrance, and she slowly sunk down onto it, making us both moan in pleasure. She was warm and soft and so tight my brain short-circuited at the jolt of pleasure that shot up my spine.

"West..." she breathed, fingers digging into my shoulders as she lifted up, before sliding back down on my shaft, making me groan against her shoulder. My fingers curled around her waist, lifting her as she pushed up again only to drop back down even harder, letting me fill every inch of her.

"I'm not going to last if you keep taking my cock like that, baby."

"That's the whole point," she said through panting breaths. "I want you to come so hard you forget your own name."

I slid my hands up her sides, gliding them over her chest to cup her tits. I brought one to my mouth, tongue sweeping and sucking over the pink bud.

She leaned into me, her hips thrusting faster. "That feels so good... yes... yes... yes." She clung to me, throwing her head back as she bounced in my lap.

It felt so good I was seconds away from coming. But I wanted to get her off first.

Sliding a hand over her ass, I gave it a firm smack. She yelped, eyes fixing on me with heady need.

"Do it again," she demanded.

I obeyed, slapping her perfect ass cheek a second time,

the whack filling the room. She moaned against my throat, tongue running over my ear.

"Oh my fucking God, do that again and I'm going to come," she said between panted breaths.

I wrapped an arm around her waist, pulling her tight against me as she moved up and down, my shaft pulsing with every thrust. Then I pulled back my hand, smacking her ass harder than before.

Her fingers tightened on my shoulders, her hips rocking desperately. Then she tensed, her entire body going taut with pleasure.

"Oh God, oh God, oh God," she said, her whole body trembling.

"That's it, baby. Give it to me."

I smacked her ass again and she whimpered, my hand massaging the soft flesh.

"West, I'm going to come. Oh my god!"

I bounced her on my cock, closing my mouth over hers and swallowing her moan, my own orgasm building at the base of my spine, ready to shoot.

Fuck, she was the hottest thing I'd ever had riding me. And I never wanted her to stop.

* * *

Monty had worked me so hard I might have pulled a muscle and that was an injury I never wanted to have to explain to Coach. It was totally worth it though, to have her straddling me, her incredible body in my hands, while she rode my cock to two orgasms.

We were wrapped around each other in my bed, Monty still naked and tucked under my arm, her leg thrown over my waist and her fingers trailing over my abs.

"So, Davis has roped us all into playing trivia or something at O'Reilly's next Saturday night," I said, tugging the blanket up over both of us.

She pulled a face. "Davis is into trivia?"

"The girl he's trying to bed this week is hosting it. But the only way it'll be halfway bearable is if you're there to make out with me and I can sneak looks at your amazing tits all night."

She laughed, swatting at me. I grabbed her wrist and pulled her on top of me, her warm body pressed against mine making my cock harden between us again.

My hands skimmed up and down her back, dipping low to caress her ass.

Fuck, she was perfect. I couldn't believe how close I'd come to missing out on this.

"I can't next weekend, I'm going away," she said, and my hands stalled.

"Away where?"

"I have a writer's conference in Toledo. My bus leaves Friday, but I'll be back on Sunday. You want to grab dinner then?"

It wasn't that I was such a clingy boyfriend already that I couldn't handle her going away, but now that I had her, I wanted her all the time. In the morning, after practice, between classes. Every moment we weren't busy doing something else, I wanted her right here and really, really naked.

But I wouldn't stand in the way of her goals either.

"Take my car, it's better than the bus. I'll catch a ride with Bant for the weekend."

Her eyes lit up. "Are you sure?"

I nodded, gripping the back of her head to bring her mouth to mine.

"I'm sure," I said. "Got to look after my girl."

She grinned at me, a devilish glint in her eye. "You just gave me two orgasms in a row, I'd never claim you don't take care of me."

I wrapped an arm around her waist, rolling her onto her back.

"Then how about we try for number three?"

Chapter Twenty-Three

MONTY

It was halfway through the third quarter and West had been subbed for a break after scoring an epic three-pointer. He was playing like a beast, owning both ends of the court. I'd say it was because he knew there was a scout from Buffalo in the crowd, but he always played this way. An off game for West was a good game for other players and I knew he could keep it up for their next game against Nebraska, when Coach Sorensen had gotten word that three NBA scouts would be watching.

It was just a shame I had to leave when Pierson was dominating.

"Okay, I better go," I said to Imogen and Stella.

If I waited any longer, I'd be getting to my hotel room in Toledo way too late.

I was excited about this writer's conference. One of my favorite authors was doing a seminar, followed by a writing workshop, but tickets were first-come-first-served. I had to get to the conference early on Saturday morning if I hoped to snag myself a spot, which was why I'd organized to leave tonight and stay in a hotel for the weekend.

"Be safe, call us tomorrow," Stella said, getting to her feet and pulling me into a hug.

Imogen joined in, wrapping her arms around both of us. "Don't have too much fun without us."

"You two are acting like I'm going off to war. I'll only be gone two nights."

"It's two nights too long," Stella said.

I waved, starting down the steps of the bleachers. West glanced over his shoulder from the bench, coming over to meet me at the edge of the court.

He cupped my face in both hands, kissing me soft and slow, teasing me with his tongue.

"Hurry back," he said, that suggestive twinkle in his eye.

Ugh. If he didn't have a game right now I'd force him into the car with me so we could fool around in my hotel room every moment I wasn't at the conference.

I was well and truly addicted to him.

"And drive safe," he said, giving my ass a squeeze.

"I will, given you're lending me your fancy car. Are you sure you're okay to catch a ride with one of the guys after the game?"

"Yeah, I'm good. Text me when you get there." He dipped his mouth to mine one last time. "I miss you already, babe."

"WRIGHT!" Coach Sorensen shouted. "Get your goddamn head in the game!"

I shoved him away. "Go win this thing before Coach reams us both."

He jogged back to the bench, Coach leaning down to mutter a few choice words in his ear.

I rounded the edge of the court and pushed out the back

doors of the stadium, striding down the path towards the parking lot.

West's car was thankfully close to the door, but the quiet dark of the lot still put me on edge.

I gripped the keys between my fingers, letting out a small sigh of relief as I reached the car.

But the scuff of a shoe behind me made my neck prickle and my shoulders tense. I tried to turn to scan the parking lot and reassure myself I was being paranoid when strong arms wrapped around from behind.

I tried to scream but something wet slid over my mouth and nose, muffling it.

The smell of chemicals invaded my senses and my vision tinged white at the edges, West's keys slipping from my fingers.

* * *

I woke to a car rumbling beneath me.

My head felt heavy, and my stomach was rolling like I might be sick. I could barely open my eyes.

I managed to lift my head, blinking to clear my clouded vision.

It was still dark outside, the landscape whizzing by as the car rocketed along a freeway.

"You're awake."

I turned my head, the movement sending pain shooting through my skull.

My eyes widened. "Alec?" I croaked. "What are we doing here? Where are we going?"

"Home."

Sitting up in my seat, I gripped the door handle as we

swerved around the car in front of us. My stomach rolled again.

Hell, why was I tired? So, so tired.

"Home? I don't... what..."

I squinted, trying to clear my fogged head. We were headed for Connecticut?

"We just need to get back home, and everything will get back on track," Alec muttered. "Just get back home and it will all be fine."

He glanced at me, reaching out a hand to grip my thigh and I flinched, pulling away from him, but it was like my body moved in slow motion.

What had he done to me?

"Alec, listen to me—"

"No, you listen to me," Alec said, and I flinched at his harsh tone.

His agitation made him swerve into the next lane. He gripped the steering wheel, hauling it back in the opposite direction. "You screwing around on me is over. You had your fun and now it's done. We're going home where we can be together, without any distractions, and everything will be just like it was. We'll be happy, Monty, you'll see."

"Going home isn't going to change anything." I tried to keep the quiver from my voice. The weight of what had happened—what was happening—sinking in. "I don't want this, Alec."

"YES, YOU DO!" His face twisted with rage.

He pressed down on the accelerator and the car surged forward. He spun the wheel to the left to miss a dark grey minivan in our path.

I squeezed my eyes shut, ignoring the way it made my head spin. I didn't want to die like this.

Alec had jumped me outside the stadium and thrown

me in his car.

The stadium.

West.

I felt my pockets for my phone.

"I took it," Alec said, glancing between me and the road.

"Please give me my phone back." I swallowed against the fear roiling inside me. "I need to call my mom, Alec."

He shook his head. "We'll be home soon, you'll see her then."

Home soon? How far had we come? It was at least ten hours from Michigan to Connecticut and it was still pitch-black outside.

I glanced at the clock on the console. *12.04am.*

It had been just shy of two hours since I'd left the basketball stadium.

"Please take me back. We don't need to go home. Let's go back to Pierson and talk about this."

Alec shook his head. "No."

"Why? I don't want to be here, Alec. I'm scared."

His gaze narrowed, and he glanced at me before returning his gaze to the road.

"You have nothing to be afraid of with me. I would never hurt you, Monty. I'm saving you."

I sucked in a shaky breath. Trying to reason with him was the only way I was going to get out of this car. If I could get him to slow down, to pull over, I might have a chance of outrunning him if I moved fast.

Nothing about my sluggish head or rolling stomach screamed fast, but I had to try. At the speed he was driving, we'd be lucky to make it to Connecticut in one piece.

He glanced my way again and the manic glint in his eye made my stomach tighten. "Alec... I'm scared. Please slow down."

His foot came off the pedal ever so slightly and the car slowed.

"Please, let me out. I don't want to go home. My friends, they're going to be worried about me when I don't text them."

"They don't care about you, they let you walk through that dark parking lot on your own. They didn't care that you were going to drive through the night to another state by yourself. I'd never let that happen."

I stilled. How did he know where I'd been going? The only people who'd known about my trip to Toledo were Imogen, Stella, West and my professor. I hadn't even told my mom.

"Please Alec, just let me call someone."

"You want to call *him*, don't you?"

His expression twisted with rage, and I rushed to shake my head.

"He doesn't love you, Monty. Not like I do. I'm taking care of you. All he cares about is shooting hoops and getting laid."

It was a totally unfair assessment of West. He was so much more than some jock looking for a good time. He was thoughtful and attentive and sweet. But revealing any of those things to Alec would only rile him.

"I don't want to call him. I want to call my mom."

Alec shook his head. "I told you that you can talk to her when we get home."

"She's going to be worried. Just let me call her and tell her we're on our way."

He glanced at me again.

"Please Alec, I'll feel so much better when my mom knows we're coming. She'll want to make sure she has everything ready when we get there."

His death grip on the steering wheel loosened. "You want us to stay with your parents?"

This entire situation was so messed up, but it was clear Alec had passed the point of sanity. The only way to reach him now was going to be to play along.

I swallowed hard. "Yes."

His right hand left the steering wheel to slide my phone from his pocket, and I almost sobbed with relief when he handed it over.

I had two texts from Imogen and four from West, as well as a bunch of missed calls from both of them and Stella.

Imogen: *Miss you already, boo x*

West: *Hey babe, hope you're enjoying your road trip and rocking those tunes loud. We won the game. Catching a ride home with Davis. Can't stop thinking about you x*

West: *I'm at a party watching Bant and Imogen go at each other. It's only a matter of time until they get naked. Wish you were here so we could get naked.*

West: *Babe, one of the freshmen on the team just sent me a picture of my Rover in the parking lot behind the stadium. Did you decide to take the bus?*

West: *Monty, where are you?*

Imogen: *Hey, call me. We're all freaking out. I'm sure you're fine, but let us know, okay? xxx*

Tears filled my eyes, my hands shaking as I tried to unlock my phone to send an SOS.

"What's wrong with you?" Alec demanded.

"I... nothing," I said, tilting my phone screen away from him.

"You're trying to text *him,* aren't you?"

I shook my head, but Alec snatched the phone from my hand, and I let out a desperate, anguished cry. That phone was my only lifeline.

"Alec, please! I only want to call my mom!"

"I don't believe you!"

He stepped on the accelerator, the speed rising with his fury. With one hand on the wheel, he scrolled through my phone with the other, the car swerving all over the road.

His expression darkened like a thundercloud. "You slept with him."

I flinched away from him, my heart hammering in my chest. "No, I didn't..."

"YOU HAD SEX WITH HIM!" Alec screamed, the car narrowly missing a sedan in the lane next to us.

I shook my head, panic rising in my throat and tears sliding down my cheeks.

"Why the hell would you fuck him? Why would you do that, Monty?"

I bit the inside of my cheek, too afraid to speak, my whole body trembling with fear.

"How could you betray me like that?" Alec glanced at

me then back at the road, his fingers gripping the leather of the steering wheel. "How am I supposed to trust you again when you lie to me, Monty?"

Tears slid down my cheeks. I was going to die here. If Alec didn't slow down, he was going to kill us both and he didn't seem to care at all.

"I was so patient. I waited and waited for you to come back to me. I let you have your fun with that man-whore jock, while trying to show you that it was me you're meant to be with. He doesn't care about you; can't you see that? I'm the one for you. I'll always take care of you."

He reached out to stroke my hair and I whimpered, shaking all over as he darted around traffic, driving with one hand.

Please don't let me die like this. Please don't let me die.

He gripped my chin, forcing me to look at him. "We're perfect for each other, Monty. I love you. So goddamn much."

His hold on me tightened and I winced. "Alec, please watch the road."

He glanced at the highway in front of us, then back at me, his gaze dropping to my mouth. "God, I've missed you."

He leaned towards me, the car swerving with him.

"Alec, no!"

The car hit the siding of the highway, scraping along it. Alec let go of me to yank the wheel in the opposite direction, only he pulled too hard, and the car fishtailed, spinning around and careening straight at the concrete wall dividing the road.

I screamed, but it was drowned out by the screech of tires as we slammed into it.

Chapter Twenty-Four

WEST

Where the hell was she?

I paced my room praying for someone's phone to ring. Imogen and Stella sat side by side on the small couch by the window, Stella gnawing on her thumbnail as she stared, seemingly at nothing. Van leaned against my desk idly tapping his fingers against the timber, while Bant was laid out on the bed.

The party celebrating the team's win tonight raged downstairs but none of us cared. None of it mattered when Monty wasn't answering our calls.

"Why hasn't she texted anyone back?" I said to no one in particular, running a hand through my hair.

"She might just be driving and hasn't checked her phone," Van offered, glancing at me and then the others.

Stella shook her head. "Something isn't right. I can feel it. Why would she leave West's keys on the ground in the parking lot? Anyone could have picked them up and driven off with his car. Monty wouldn't do that."

One of the freshmen on the team had texted me after the game telling me my car was still in the lot. I'd caught a ride home with Davis, and we'd left through the side entrance, totally bypassing the main lot. I should have checked for my car before I left to make sure she'd gotten away okay. Then we would have known earlier that something was up.

When I'd texted the freshmen back and asked him to check out my ride, he said he'd found the keys near the driver's side door.

Bant sat up. "What if—"

"Don't say it," I growled.

He raised both hands. "I'm not trying to stir shit, but someone has to say it. It's a possibility."

"What? Alec?" Stella asked, her green eyes wide.

The two girls gave each other a look I couldn't stand the sight of. They were freaking out just as much as I was but trying to keep a lid on it.

"Anyone know where he lives?" Van asked.

Imogen got to her feet in a rush. "Yeah, I do."

The walk across campus was the longest fifteen minutes of my life. We reached Corinell House, one of the smaller dorms, just as a group of girls were leaving.

"Which way?" I asked Imogen, snagging the door and holding it open.

Imogen turned down a hallway to the right, stopping at the elevator and we rode it to the third floor.

"What if he's home? Then what?" Stella asked.

"Then we wait," I said, hoping like hell Alec was there when we knocked on the door. If he was home, that meant Monty was likely safe and Van was right—she probably just wasn't checking her phone while she was on the road to Toledo.

But if he wasn't...

I clenched my fists at my sides, following Imogen down the hall. I didn't want to think about what it meant if Alec was gone too.

Imogen stopped and pounded on a dorm room door. It swung open, revealing the tall guy who'd been at Ruby's with Alec.

"Alec home?" Van asked, peering behind him.

The guy frowned. "No."

"Do you know where he is?"

The guy shook his head. "I haven't seen him since this morning. He said something about going home for a while."

Silence hung over our group.

"Thanks." Imogen turned on her heel for the elevator.

We followed, no one uttering a word until we were back outside, the quiet stillness of the campus matching the mood hanging over us.

"He's with Monty. He's taken her," Imogen said, and Stella whimpered beside her.

"You don't know that for sure," Bant said.

Imogen turned on him.

"Oh, no? Monty has been my best friend since we were six. Even if she were driving, she wouldn't ignore our panicked texts and calls like this. She's more considerate than that. Alec has been stalking her for more than a year. He's finally snapped and taken her back to Connecticut."

"Why would he suddenly boil over into full blown abduction? What set him off?" Van asked.

She pointed at me, and I reared back. "You think this is my fault?"

"Not at all. But I think Alec does. He clearly came to Pierson to get her back, only Monty didn't want anything to do with him. Now that she's with you, he's likely convinced himself that you're the problem and if he can just get her away from you, she'll come back to him."

If Imogen's theory was correct, then Alec was more deluded than any of us had realized. If he'd so much as touched her...

I paced the floor, feeling like a caged animal. "We have to find them."

"How the hell are we supposed to do that?" Stella asked, her voice shaking. "We have no way of knowing which roads they might have taken."

Van put an arm around her shoulders to comfort her and she leaned into him.

"Fuck!" I turned away from them, running my hands through my hair.

I never should have let her leave the stadium on her own at night. Not when I knew how freaked out she was about Alec. I was supposed to protect her, and I'd left her exposed and alone.

"Why is West so worked up?" Stella asked Van. "We're all worried about Monty."

Van glanced at me. "Because he's in love with her."

I knew he'd suspected how I really felt about Monty. Hell, he probably knew it before I did. Van and I had been teammates and roommates since freshman year. He could read me better than anyone. And he was right.

I was in love with Monty.

And right now, I'd do just about anything to get her back.

"I thought they were faking it," Bant said, his stunned expression a match for Stella's.

"Of course he's in love with her. You'd have to be blind not to notice," Imogen said, levelling Bant with a flat stare.

Stella turned to her with wide eyes, Van's arm slipping from her shoulders. "You knew?"

Imogen's expression softened. "It's not like he told me or anything. I knew it that night in the bar when he knocked back that girl with the giant chest."

"How giant are we talking?" Bant asked, earning him a collective groan from the group.

Van clapped him on the shoulder. "Dude, now is not the time to think with your dick."

"Wow," Stella said, clearly still floored. "Kissing random guys on the quad really paid off for Monty. Maybe I should try it." Her gaze landed on me. "Does Monty know?"

I blew out a long breath and shook my head.

"We could start driving to Connecticut," Van said. "But without knowing which roads they've taken we've got no way to track them."

Imogen let out a gasp. "Oh my god... the tracking app." Her eyes widened. "We need to go back to our dorm. I know how we might be able to find her."

We were back in the girls' common room ten minutes later, Imogen's laptop opened on the kitchenette counter.

"Monty and I have a tracking app set up for each other, we've just never really used it," Imogen said, logging in. "If her phone is still turned on, this app should be able to locate her."

"Why would you need to track each other?" Bant asked, biting into an apple he'd swiped from the fridge.

Imogen shrugged. "We set it up when we were in high school, so we always knew where the other one was."

I leaned over her shoulder. "So can you find her?"

Worry pinched her expression. "It's searching. I have no idea if she still has it set up or even turned on." She bit her lip like she was fighting back tears. "I should have thought of it earlier."

I squeezed her shoulder. "This isn't your fault, Imogen."

She nodded, both of us staring at the screen, waiting for it to refresh.

The laptop pinged, a blue dot suddenly appearing on the map on screen.

"She's on the Ohio turnpike," Imogen said, standing tall. "I'll drive."

Chapter Twenty-Five

MONTY

My entire body felt like it was on fire.

Everything hurt.

My ears were ringing so loud I couldn't think, couldn't feel, couldn't move. I tried to clamp my hands over them to stop it, but I couldn't make my limbs move the way I wanted them to.

Pain shot through me, and I groaned in the darkness, forcing my eyes open.

The concrete siding of the highway stared back at me, the entire front of the car a crumpled mess. The windshield was shattered, and the roof had partially caved on my side so I was scrunched in my seat, the siding so close I could reach out and touch it.

Claustrophobia hit me like a tidal wave, the ringing in my ears dulling everything around me. My throat and collarbone burned with the sting of the seatbelt and the smell of gas hit my nose, making me gag.

That was bad, right? Surely that was bad.

I have to get out of here.

Gripping the dashboard, I slid to my left to free my legs from the wreckage, an agonized cry escaping me at the searing pain in my torso. When I tried to shift my feet, a sharp burst of pain shot through my right ankle, travelling all the way up my leg into my hip.

Holy shit. That hurt. Why did that hurt so much?

I pushed through the pain, leaning further to my left until my legs swung free, and I dragged myself up and out the front window, my good foot connecting with something as I pulled it through behind me.

A low groan sounded from inside the car, my body suddenly vibrating with fear.

Alec.

He was still strapped into the front seat, his eyes closed, a river of blood running down his face.

I scrambled away from him, rolling across the crumpled hood and hitting the ground hard. Gravel bit into my palms and arms as I dragged myself away from the car. My ears were still ringing *so loud* and my head pounded. My leg, my side, my head, my shoulder all hurt, every inch of me moving pain.

I could hear voices, but the ringing just wouldn't stop.

"Miss? Miss, can you hear me?" a voice said, muffled like I was swimming underwater. "Miss, you're injured. Please stay still."

Opening my mouth, I tried to form words, but only rasping sounds came out.

Hands gripped me, trying to roll me over on the ground but I pushed them away.

Up, up, up, I had to get up. Get away from the car.

Planting both palms on the ground, I pushed up, only to fall again.

"Miss, you really shouldn't try to walk."

"I've called 911, the paramedics are on their way," another voice said.

I tried to get up again, this time using something solid to help me. A car, I think. I managed to get upright, only to stumble, arms catching me around the waist.

"You're okay," a voice soothed. "You're safe now."

I didn't feel safe. Not when Alec was in that car, and everything hurt like this.

I stared at the highway in front of me. It was at a standstill, cars stopped haphazardly across the lanes.

"You're okay, everything is okay now," the voice said. "The paramedics will be here soon."

I turned to stare at the voice beside me. An older man stared back at me, his eyes wide and... concerned? His arm was still around my waist, and we leaned against another car.

"What..." I croaked.

"Don't try to speak." His voice was kind. Soothing. "You were in a very bad accident. Help will be here soon."

I nodded, my head so heavy.

A siren wailed in the distance, growing closer. My head lolled to the side.

My skull, my torso, my ankle, all throbbed with pain so sharp and fierce it made my vision tinge white at the edges.

A searing full body ache overwhelmed me, and I slumped against the man.

Chapter Twenty-Six

WEST

We piled into Imogen's Ford Escape, Van and Bant practically folding themselves in half to fit in the backseat on either side of Stella.

"You couldn't spring for a bigger car?" Bant asked, shifting uncomfortably.

"I didn't plan on having three giants taking a ride when I factored in the size at purchase," Imogen cut back.

She floored it, merging onto the freeway to a chorus of honks. She was a maniac behind the wheel, but I'd expect nothing less from Imogen.

"I'd like to get there alive," Van said, but Imogen ignored him, darting in and out of traffic to get around cars she declared "dickheads who can't drive".

More than an hour of tense silence passed, everyone lost in their own heads over what we might find when he reached the Ohio Turnpike. Imogen had synced the tracking app on her phone with Monty's location. The blue dot on the map hadn't moved since we left the dorms.

Where the hell had Alec taken her?

Imogen slowed, and I leaned forward in my seat, traffic backed up for miles in front of us. And far off in the distance, emergency lights flashed.

Imogen swore at the sight, pulling the car onto the shoulder.

I didn't wait for the others, unfolding myself from the car and bolting down the emergency lane, Bant calling after me. My feet pounded the pavement, passing car after car after car filled with impatient drivers at a standstill on the freeway.

When I finally reached the flashing lights, I didn't stop, passing parked police cars and ambulances and darting around vehicles, only to stall at the nightmare laid out in front of me.

Debris was strewn across all four lanes of the highway, cars haphazardly parked in the road. And there, in the center lane, crumpled against the concrete siding, was a silver Volkswagen.

The front windshield was blown to pieces and the remnants of the two front windows scattered on the ground. The car had clearly hit the barrier head-on. The hood was mangled and the roof partially caved in.

I stared, stunned. There was surely no way anyone had survived that.

"Sir," someone called to me nearby. "Sir, you can't be here, you need to move back behind the police vehicles."

I barely heard them though, unable to tear my eyes from the mangled mess in front of me.

Please God, don't let her have been in there.

Footsteps pounded behind me, Imogen and Van stopping at my side, Stella and Bant just behind.

"Imogen, tell me that's not Alec's car," I said.

One look at her pale, horrified face as she stared at the crumpled mess in front of us told me everything I needed to know. Despair and rage warred inside me.

"Oh my god, no," Stella said, tears streaming down her cheeks.

Van folded her in his arms.

"Excuse me," a police officer said, coming to stand in front of us so he couldn't be ignored. "You can't be here. You need to get back behind the cars."

I waited for Imogen to mobilize, to shout at him that her best friend might have been in that car and demand answers. But she stood, frozen, staring at the car like her world had just been torn apart.

"Please, we knew the girl in the car. Did she survive?" Stella asked.

The officer's expression softened. "The driver and the young woman have been taken to hospital."

I ran a hand through my hair, tugging on it. "Is she okay?"

The officer sighed. "They both suffered very serious injuries, especially the driver."

"I don't care about that piece of shit, what about the girl?"

He looked momentarily startled by my lack of regard for Alec's wellbeing. "You know her?"

"She's our best friend," Stella said through her tears. "Can you at least tell us what hospital?"

The officer glanced over his shoulder, then back at Stella. "She's been taken to Bellevue, along with the driver." Someone called his name and he backed away. "Please move yourselves back behind the police cars."

I nodded, still not listening, my eyes trained on the wreck.

"You're friends with the girl?" a man asked, edging around a nearby car.

He was older, maybe in his sixties, and his shirt was spattered with small drops of blood.

"Yes," Bant said, eyeing the guy.

"I'm Orlando, I helped her after she pulled herself from the car. I waited with her until the paramedics arrived."

My eyes widened. Not only had Monty survived the crash, she had somehow managed to free herself from *that*?

"The boy was unconscious behind the wheel, stayed that way until the paramedics took him."

When none of us offered a response, he went on.

"The girl was pretty beat up but she was alert, even tried to talk to me. Then all of a sudden she collapsed in my arms."

My jaw tightened. "What happened?"

"I'm sorry, that's all I know. The paramedics took her away soon after, I really hope she's okay."

"Thank you," Stella said, smiling sadly.

I turned to Imogen. "Im, we need to go. We should be at the hospital."

She didn't respond, staring at the wreckage without really seeing it.

I gripped her shoulders. "Imogen? Imogen, look at me."

Her gaze slid to me, her brow pinching.

"We need to go. Monty's in the hospital."

She nodded, glancing back at the car, until Stella came and took her hand.

The five of us ran back to Imogen's car. We found the doors sitting open, the keys still in the ignition, abandoned in our haste to get to Monty.

"I... I don't think I can drive," Imogen said.

"I'll do it." Van slid into the driver's seat.

Imogen and Stella climbed into the backseat with Bant and I took the front.

Pulling an illegal U-turn through a ditch, Van sped along the shoulder on the other side of the highway, swerving to take the first exit he could find. No one questioned it. None of us wanted to sit in traffic while Monty could be dying in a hospital somewhere, totally alone.

"She's not going to die," Stella muttered quietly to Imogen in the backseat, stroking her hair.

It took twenty-five torturous minutes to make it to the hospital, Imogen, Stella and I tumbling from the car in a rush as soon as we stopped.

"Bant and I will find a place to park, and we'll meet you in there. We'll come find you," Van called.

The three of us rushed through the emergency waiting room to the nurse's station.

"Emily Montgomery. They brought her here in an ambulance in the last few hours, she was in a car accident," Imogen said, tears pooling in her eyes.

"Are you next of kin?" the nurse asked, eyes landing on each of us.

"I'm her best friend, I've known her since we were kids," Imogen said. "She's like a sister to me."

Stella nodded. "I'm her other best friend."

The nurse looked to me.

"I'm her boyfriend."

"Please, she was in a car accident," Imogen said. "We've just come from the scene. We have to know she's okay."

She turned to Stella and I, tears falling freely down her cheeks. "She has to be okay."

The grief written on her face was enough to break me, and I pulled her into a hug, the backs of my eyes burning hot.

"She can't die," Imogen muttered against my chest.

The nurse's brow pinched in sympathy. "Take a seat, let me see what I can find out."

We walked to the nearest cluster of chairs near a mother and toddler, who appeared to have a marble stuck up his nose, and a man with a severely infected tattoo of a rabbit on his quad.

"She's going to be okay, Im," Stella soothed as they both took a seat.

I couldn't sit. If I sat I was going to break something. Smash something into a thousand tiny pieces at the life-threatening situation Monty had been caught up in. She didn't deserve this. Didn't deserve to be stalked on campus, or made to feel unsafe in her dorm room, or have to fear for her life leaving a basketball game.

I scrubbed both hands over my face.

Fuck.

I just wanted to see her. To hold her hand and know that she was going to be fine. Not knowing if she was okay or if she ever would be again was killing me.

After what felt like a year, the large double doors at the side of the room opened and the nurse from the desk appeared.

"Emily Montgomery's friends," she called, motioning us over. "Come with me."

Stella and Imogen were on their feet, trailing me across the room. We followed the nurse through doors that opened into a long, wide hallway.

"We got in touch with your friend's parents. They're on their way. They gave me permission to talk to you. Your friend is in surgery. She has several injuries, including several cracked ribs that punctured a lung. They're repairing them now."

Imogen sucked in a sharp breath.

"We won't know more until she's out. You can sit in the waiting room outside recovery. The doctor will come and speak to you when they're done."

She took us in the elevator one floor up, leading us to a smaller waiting room off another wide hallway. The hospital was a maze we'd likely never find our way out of. But it didn't matter to me, I didn't plan on leaving. Not without Monty.

"Thank you," Stella said to the nurse. "We're so grateful for your help."

She nodded and disappeared.

Van and Bant eventually turned up, and the five of us spent hours waiting with nothing to do but worry.

The dark sky outside slowly morphed into day, a blue cloudless sky taking its place, totally at odds with the mood hanging over us in the waiting room.

The surgeon emerged a few hours later, dressed in teal scrubs.

"You're here for Emily Montgomery?" she asked, kind eyes sweeping each of us.

Imogen and I got to our feet.

"Yes," we said in unison.

"The surgery went well, all things considered. Emily has two cracked ribs, one of which punctured her lung, what we call a pneumothorax. We had to go in surgically to repair the damage. We're confident she'll heal, but the tube will need to remain for a couple of days to ensure her lung repairs as it should."

It was one thing to hear about these kinds of injuries on TV, but hearing them being used to describe Monty made my chest tighten.

"She has a burn on her neck from the seatbelt, as well as

some bruising around her hips. There's a fracture in her right ankle, which we've set. She also took a knock to the head on impact, which means she'll need to be monitored for concussion over the next several days."

Imogen faltered back a step straight into Bant who didn't hesitate, wrapping his arms around her from behind and keeping her upright. Tears tracked down her cheeks as she stared at the surgeon in disbelief.

"It's quite remarkable that Emily managed to pull herself from the wreckage with those injuries. She's one tough young woman."

"Th-thank you," Imogen said. "Thank you for saving her."

The surgeon gave us a small smile. "She'll rest here for the next few hours at least so we can monitor her, then we'll move her to her own room. We have high hopes for her recovery, but she's got some work to do first. Right now, we wait."

"Can we see her?" I asked, trying to keep the desperation from my voice.

The surgeon shook her head. "She needs time to recover from surgery. Once they move her to a room, you'll be able to see her."

"Thank you, doctor."

Nodding, she disappeared back through the double doors.

Monty was in there somewhere, lying in a bed alone.

I turned for the windows, running my hands through my hair. A few hours. That's all I had to wait. Just a few more hours and then I'd be able to see her.

Van wandered over, squeezing my shoulder. "You okay?"

I shook my head. "Not at all."

"It's sounds grim, but Monty's tough. She'll get back on her feet."

My gaze slid to his. "I'm glad you're optimistic about it. I can't stop thinking about what she must have been feeling being stuck in that car with him."

"That piece of shit has some serious issues. There's no way he'll avoid jail for this."

The thought didn't offer much comfort, because it wouldn't help Monty heal any faster.

My chin dropped to my chest, emotion burning behind my eyes. Losing her right now, when we'd only just found our way to each other, wasn't an option.

I was in love with her.

And I should have told her that when I had the chance.

Another two hours passed.

We sat around the quiet waiting room listening to the nurses bustle around and the distant beep of hospital machines. We talked occasionally, but none of us had much to say. Bant got snacks and drinks from the vending machine down the hall, but none of us were that hungry either.

Finally, a nurse in navy scrubs appeared, telling us Monty had been moved to a room. She led us through the maze of the hospital, taking the elevator up two floors. After checking in at the nurse's station, she led us to the last door on the left at the end of the hall.

"She's pretty bruised up. She's on oxygen and the beeping machine she's hooked up to is monitoring her heart rate. Seeing her like this might be a little overwhelming, but I assure you, she's doing okay. They wouldn't have moved her up here if she wasn't. She's sleeping now and she'll be in and out of it over the next couple of days, given the high dosage of pain meds she's on. So don't expect much from her right now."

Imogen and Stella shared a glance, taking each other's hands. The nurse opened the door and ushered us in, closing it again behind us.

The room was mostly dark, only a slither of daylight cracking through the closed curtains. It was quiet, save for the constant beep of the heart rate monitor.

But it was the girl in the bed I couldn't take my eyes off.

"Oh my god," Imogen said quietly. She slipped her hand in Monty's. "What has he done to you?"

Stella moved to Imogen's side. "Hey Monts, we missed you. We just want you to know we're here."

Monty didn't stir, the drugs keeping her under, and I catalogued every inch of the girl I was in love with.

Her head was wrapped in a bandage that crossed above her left eye. There was a patch on her neck from the seatbelt burn. Her face was so pale, almost grey, and even with her dark lashes fanning over her cheeks while she slept, there was no hiding the dark circles under her eyes.

I rounded the bed, pulling up a chair to sit beside her and taking her hand.

The last image I had of her filled my mind—the way she'd smiled at me at the game when I'd kissed her goodbye.

I'd been a lucky fool when she'd chosen to kiss me that day on the quad. And when I got her back, I'd spend every day making sure she knew how much she'd come to mean to me.

Monty was everything I'd never known I needed.

Now what I needed was for her to wake up.

* * *

Bant and Van left, taking Imogen and Stella with them. The girls promised to return with a bag for me given I was still wearing the sweats I'd changed into after the game last night.

I stayed exactly where I'd been from the moment I'd stepped through the door. Next to Monty.

I'd wasted so much time with her trying to kid myself about my true feelings for her. All because of my stupid hang-ups from my parents and because I wasn't sure if she wanted me. But seeing her lying in a hospital bed had given me all kinds of perspective.

I loved her and I wanted the chance to tell her.

Imogen and Stella returned several hours later, dropping a bag at my feet.

I'd nodded off, my neck stiff and sore from falling asleep in the chair with my head on Monty's bed. I glanced at the clock on the wall.

"No change?" Stella asked.

I shook my head, just as the door opened and a man and a woman hurried into the room.

"Oh, my baby," the woman said, staring at Monty's sleeping form, tears filling her eyes. She had the same color hair and long legs as Monty.

"Jane, Stuart," Imogen said, tears leaking from the corners of her eyes. She rushed them and they pulled her into a double hug.

"We spoke to the doctors on the way in. How is she?" Mrs. Montgomery asked.

She turned to the bed, her eyes filling with tears as she stroked Monty's arm. Mr. Montgomery moved to the other side, brushing a hand over Monty's forehead as she slept.

"She stirred once, about an hour ago. Other than that, she's been out of it," I said quietly.

Mr. Montgomery turned to assess me, and I stood, offering him my hand. "I'm West Wright, sir."

He took my hand, shaking it firmly.

"West is Monty's boyfriend," Imogen offered.

"Boyfriend?" The Montgomerys exchanged a look of surprise.

"It's nice to meet you both," I said.

"You too, son," Mr. Montgomery said, but his eyes had already returned to his daughter.

I nodded, taking up a place by the window next to Stella, suddenly feeling like I didn't belong here. Not when Monty's parents had clearly known nothing about me.

Stella gave me a small smile, patting my knee. "She'd want you here. Don't you worry about that."

Chapter Twenty-Seven

WEST

I woke to the sound of a door slamming. I startled, sitting up from where I'd fallen asleep on the small couch by the window in Monty's room, my feet hanging awkwardly over the sides.

"Sorry," Mr. Montgomery said, pulling a face. "I tried to shut it quietly, but it was difficult with these." He motioned with the two cups of coffee in his hands, extending one to me.

I sat up, swinging my feet onto the floor and accepting it. "Thank you."

"No problem. You look like you could use it." He took a seat on the couch beside me.

Monty's parents had been alternating who stayed at the hospital, so one of them was always with her while the other went back to their hotel to get a couple of hours sleep or shower and change.

But I hadn't left. I'd lost track of the hours I'd spent staring at Monty while she slept.

The doctors had slowly been decreasing her pain medication over the past twenty-four hours to help her wake. Now we just had to wait for Monty to be ready.

"How long have you two been seeing each other?" Mr. Montgomery asked, taking a sip of his coffee.

"Not long, only a couple of months."

"But you haven't left her side since we got here..."

There was nothing accusatory about the way he said it, just observational.

I watched Monty from across the room, her hair fanned out on the pillow around her. One of the nurses had come in to remove the bandage from her head a few hours ago and her face had regained some color.

"It may have only been a few months, but Monty means a lot to me."

Mr. Montgomery gave me a nod of approval.

"I watch enough college ball to know you've got quite a future ahead of you."

I sipped my coffee, the heat burning my throat slightly. "Thank you, sir."

"Is the NBA the end goal?"

"I've been working towards it since I was eleven."

He let out a low whistle. "That's some dedication. Your folks must be proud."

"I guess so. They came to my games when I was younger but now, they're not really involved." I shrugged like it didn't matter that my parents were too caught up in their own affairs to care much about my road to the NBA. "They're busy with their own lives."

He clapped me on the shoulder. "That doesn't mean they don't love or support you. Sometimes life gets in the way and it's easy to lose touch with what really matters."

His gaze fell on his daughter.

"She never told us about the way Alec was acting and it tears me up inside," he said, his voice shaking. "I'm her father, I should have been there to protect her."

I leaned forward, elbows resting on my knees as I watched Monty, the sunlight from the window behind us slanting across the bed. Imogen had filled Mr. and Mrs. Montgomery in on everything to do with Alec. They'd known about him texting Monty last year, but they'd had no idea he'd turned up to her dorm in Florida more than once. Or any of what had gone down since she'd come to Pierson.

"She's so strong. She wanted to take care of it herself. In the beginning she wouldn't let me help her either."

I remembered that day on campus when I'd suggested we fake date and she'd knocked me back. I hadn't realized then just how deep Alec's obsession with her went. I don't think any of us realized until it escalated the way it had. I'd just known I wanted to spend time with her. To be around her. I wanted to have her look at me with that bright, wide smile of hers or laugh at something ridiculous one of my friends said.

I just wanted her healed and back to being herself.

"She didn't want to burden anyone with this," I said. "I think she blamed herself more than she blamed Alec. She wanted to fix it on her own. It was only when he started to really scare her that she let me in."

Mr. Montgomery shook his head. "I'm sad she thought she couldn't tell us. I've known that boy since he was in grade school, but there's no way I ever would have sided with him over my own daughter. I would have marched right over to his house to talk with his parents. I would have put a stop to it."

I took another sip of my coffee. "She's stubborn. She likes to do things for herself."

"She's always been that way. You've definitely got your hands full with her. In the very best way."

I smiled. "Oh, I figured that out early on. From the first moment we met, actually."

Mr. Montgomery smiled, then straightened. "Wait a minute. Doesn't Pierson have a game tomorrow?"

I nodded. I'd spoken to Coach and he'd given me approval to miss practice and the game against Nebraska, which also meant missing out on playing in front of three scouts. But there would be no point in me taking the court right now when my head wasn't in the right place. It would be right back here with Monty the entire time.

"So doesn't that mean you should be with your team?"

"Under normal circumstances, yeah." I sat tall, glancing at him. "But Monty means more to me than basketball."

He gave me a small smile, nodding in understanding.

The brush of a sheet had both our heads snapping in the direction of the bed.

"Since when?" came Monty's pained croak.

Chapter Twenty-Eight

WEST

"Sweetheart, you're awake," Mr. Montgomery said as we both rushed to the bed. "We've been worried half to death."

"Sorry, Dad," Monty said, her voice hoarse.

He shook his head, tears filling his eyes. "You have absolutely nothing to be sorry for, my girl. Nothing."

I reached for the jug on the table and poured some cool water into a cup. I fastened a top on it and handed it to her father. He swiped at the tears in his eyes with the back of his hand, then took the cup, holding the straw so Monty could drink.

When she laid back down, her eyes landed on me where I stood at the end of the bed.

"Hey."

Desperate relief flooded me at that one word.

"Hey."

There was so much I wanted to say to her, but before I

got the chance, Mrs. Montgomery came into the room. She took one look at Monty and burst into tears.

"My baby, my poor baby," Mrs. Montgomery said, coming round the side of the bed and kissing Monty's head over and over.

Monty slowly lifted a hand, her face pinched with pain, as she patted her mother's shoulder. "I'm okay, Mom."

Her mom lifted her head. "You're a fighter. I told them you'd get through this."

A crease pinched Monty's brow. "How long have I been out?"

Her parents glanced at each other. "Two days, sweetheart."

Confusion filled Monty's eyes. "Two days?"

"We drove straight here as soon as we got the call. West was already here, Imogen too. She'll be back soon," Mrs. Montgomery said. "West hasn't left. He's been here the whole time."

I shoved my hands in my pockets, and Monty's gaze landed on me again. She shifted, her eyes creasing in pain. "What about basketball?"

I shrugged. "That doesn't matter right now."

Those grey-blue eyes opened wide with surprise.

"We need to go get the doctors," Mrs. Montgomery said. "They'll want to know you're awake and what our next steps are."

Monty nodded, and Mrs. Montgomery squeezed her hand. "You don't know how happy we are to have you back, my girl."

Then she was gone.

"I think I might go help her," Mr. Montgomery said, glancing between Monty and I. He brushed a hand over Monty's arm. "We're so glad you're awake, sweetheart."

Monty gave him a small smile, and he headed for the door.

Pulling up a chair, I took Monty's hand.

"I can't believe you've been here for two straight days," she said, trying to sit up and wincing in pain.

I pushed to my feet. "Don't try to move. You're injured."

"What happened? The last thing I remember is... being in the car with Alec." Her eyes widened, like she was lost in memories in her own head. "The accident."

I nodded. "You had to have surgery."

Tears filled her eyes. "Oh my god."

"Shhh..." I stroked her cheek. "It's okay, you're fine now. You're safe. You pulled yourself from the wreck to get away from him."

"Alec," she whispered. "What happened to him?"

My jaw clenched at her question. How could she be worried about him after what he'd done to her?

She stared up at me with tortured blue-grey eyes. "Did he make it?"

I sighed. "He made it. He got out of here after a day, while your parents and I... we've been watching you fight for your life..." I swallowed hard.

She frowned, wrinkling her brow in confusion. "How have you stayed here? Coach is going to murder you. The scouts..."

I took her hand, brushing my thumb back and forth over her knuckles. "The scouts don't matter. The game doesn't matter right now."

She stared back at me, doubt coloring her expression.

"Monty, I meant it when I said that nothing is more important to me than you. There's nowhere I'd rather be than right here."

I brought her hand to my lips.

"Knowing that Alec had taken you, seeing the scene of the accident, watching you lay in this bed for two days. It helped me realize something..."

I took a deep breath knowing I had to get the words out. Words I should have said to her a long time ago.

"I love you, Monty. Wherever you are is where I'm meant to be."

Those grey-blue eyes were wider than I'd ever seen them as she stared back at me.

Then her face crumpled, and her chest heaved with a sob.

I took her face in my hands. "Babe, don't cry. Please don't cry. Shit, I shouldn't have done this now. I'm so sorry."

She swiped at her tears with her free hand. The one that had a drip tapped to the back of it, reminding us exactly where we were.

I pressed my lips to her forehead. "You don't need to say anything right now. And it doesn't matter if you don't feel the same way."

"I do..." she said, and my heart pounded in my chest.

"You do need to say something?"

She shook her head. "I do love you. I love you so much, West. And I was too afraid to tell you because I thought the moment I did, we'd be over."

I laughed. "How the hell did you not know the way I felt about you? Every time we're in the same room, I can't keep my eyes or hands off you. I can't stop thinking about you, even when I should be focused on something else like practice, or class, or a game. You're everything I've ever wanted, Monty. And I've been sitting here cursing myself for wasting time not telling you and worrying that I wouldn't get the chance."

She reached out, her hand closing around the back of my head and gently tugging me towards her.

"Monty, you're in the hospital," I teased. "I know I'm an incredible kisser, but now isn't the best time."

She gave me a weak smile. "We just said I love you, so shut up and kiss me."

I couldn't contain my grin as I dropped my mouth to hers, all the raw feelings between us pouring into it.

I loved her. So damn much.

"You kissing me on the quad might have been the best thing that ever happened to me."

Her eyes narrowed. "Might have been? Please. Jumping you was the best decision I've ever made."

Chapter Twenty-Nine

MONTY

The roar of the Pierson crowd filled the stadium and I relished being back watching West tear up the court. He was playing the game of his life in front of two NBA scouts, and Imogen, Stella and I were screaming ourselves hoarse in support.

Hernandez put up a shot and it swished in on the buzzer, the crowd turning frenzied.

It was officially half time and Pierson was up by two.

"Snack break?" Stella asked, as the players huddled.

Imogen and I nodded, following her along the edge of the court. I hobbled along in my ankle boot, the movement making my sore ribs twinge. But there was no way I was going to miss West's game. Not after he'd missed court time while sitting at my bedside in the hospital.

I'd been out a month now, and the doctors said I still had a few weeks before my ankle would be healed and the boot could come off, but I wouldn't let it hold me back.

"I'd sell a kidney for a Diet Coke right now," Imogen

said as we joined the back of the concession line. Stella and I laughed, and someone tapped me on the shoulder.

"Ms. Montgomery," my literature professor said with a wide smile. "So glad to see you back on your feet so soon."

I smiled. "Thanks, I'm feeling good."

"I don't want to interrupt but I wanted to give you the good news."

"The good news?"

She nodded, eyes crinkling with a smile. "I heard back from the short story coordinator. You placed second. You're going to be published!"

My eyes widened. "You're kidding?"

She shook her head. "I'd never kid about something as important as this. I'm sorry you never got to make it to the workshop at the conference, but I hope this makes up for it. I'm so proud of you, well done."

She gave my arm a squeeze and waved goodbye.

"Way to kill it, superstar!" Imogen said and she and Stella engulfed me in a group hug, almost making me topple.

"I can't believe I placed..."

"We can!" Stella said, squeezing my shoulder.

I couldn't believe I'd gone from lying in a hospital bed to this.

I was back on my feet and healing. West and I were more obsessed with each other than ever. And I was going to be published. All that needed to happen now was West to get drafted and life would be as sweet as it could possibly be.

Alec had been charged for his crimes and sentenced to a mental health facility. If he recovered, he'd be transferred to prison.

My family and friends had been relieved with the outcome. And I was too.

But while Alec had terrified me to the point I was still slightly scared getting into a car, there was a small part of me that hoped Alec would stay in the facility. He was sick and he deserved help, not prison. Even with everything he'd done.

"Let's get back and watch the boys bring it home," Imogen said when we'd finally made it through the concession line.

And bring it home was exactly what they did.

Pierson won by six points in a victory that was clinched in the dying minutes. They were on a hot streak that was sure to take them straight into March Madness.

I took West's hand after the game, leading him from the stadium despite his weak protests about everyone waiting for us at a victory party back at the basketball house.

"Where are we going?" he asked as we wandered, or more like hobbled, through campus.

"I'm honestly surprised you haven't worked it out yet. It's lucky you're pretty and bounce a ball so well..."

West stopped, shaking his head at the teasing insult. "If you weren't still injured, I'd throw you over my shoulder right now, carry you home and punish you in my bedroom."

"I kind of like the sound of that. Maybe you can punish me later anyway?"

West chuckled, the sound lighting me up inside.

I still couldn't believe I got to call his stupidly hot face mine. He'd stuck by my side for another three days in the hospital after I'd woken up, and he'd helped me through my recovery every day since. He'd sat by my side at Alec's hearing and met me at the end of each day on campus to carry my books for me.

I was falling more in love with him every minute we spent together.

One random kiss on the quad had changed my life in more ways than I ever could have predicted.

"Okay, this is ridiculous," West said, watching me hobble. He stopped, scooping me into his arms, honeymoon-style. I flinched at the twinge in my ribs, and his face filled with alarm. "Is this okay?"

I wrapped my arms around his neck and nodded. "This is more than okay."

He carried me up the path, letting out a groan when he realized where it was leading.

"I can't believe I didn't figure out where you were taking me," he said as we stepped into the place where it all began.

I smiled. "I thought it was only fitting that we come back here."

He put me down and I hobbled in my giant ankle boot to the exact spot we'd been standing on the quad when we first met.

"I'm honestly surprised you didn't drag Bant and Van along to reprise their roles," West said.

"I tried, they wouldn't play ball."

West chuckled.

"Really I just wanted this moment to be just for us," I said, taking his hand.

He glanced down at it, then back at me.

"Can I help you?" he asked, repeating the same words he'd asked me that day all those months ago and making me laugh.

I slid my arms around his neck.

He held my waist, blue eyes smiling down at me. "You have no idea how much I love you."

A grin spread across my face, happiness beaming out of me like a lovesick fool.

"Probably about as much as I love you."

"Yeah?"

"Of course."

His smile widened. "Well, in that case... I think you should move in with me."

My brows shot up. "You want me to move into the basketball house with you and eight of your teammates?"

He shrugged. "Yeah, why not? We'd have fun there. I've only got one more year left at Pierson, and I want to spend it with you. I want to fall asleep with you wrapped around me every night and wake up with you in my arms every morning. I want to come home every day from class or practice and know that you'll be there. I want everything with you, Monty."

I stared back at the former campus fuckboy who'd stolen my heart.

"I want that too."

And I meant it. I'd never expected that when I jumped him on the quad that it would lead to this. But now that we were here, I couldn't imagine my life without him. I'd never felt about anyone the way I felt about West and I wanted to be with him.

"So, we're doing this?" he asked, eyes lighting up.

I smiled. "Yeah, we're doing this. Let's move in together."

* * *

If you've enjoyed this book, I'd be so grateful if you could take the time to leave a review.

WANT MORE FROM PIERSON UNIVERSITY?

Read on for the first chapter of book two
SHOOTING TO WIN...

EXCERPT: SHOOTING TO WIN (PIERSON U BOOK 2)

VAN

"You're such an asshole!"

I darted out of the path of the coffee mug that came flying across the room. It hit the wall behind me and shattered, brown liquid sliding down the wall.

"I'm sorry, Belle," I said, taking a placating step towards her. "I didn't mean to hurt you."

My girlfriend—or now ex-girlfriend—shook her head, her eyes pooling with tears that made my chest clench. Just because I was breaking up with her didn't mean I wasn't hurting too or that I didn't care about her. Caring about each other was the reason we'd stuck it out this long when we both knew it wasn't working.

"I don't need to hear any more of your platitudes, Adam," Annabelle said, expression twisted with hurt. "Things have been off between us since last year and I've tried to ignore it and make it work. And now you come to me and tell me you love me but you're not *in love* with me? What kind of arrogant bullshit is that?"

I slid my hands into the pocket of my hooded sweatshirt, working to keep my emotions in check.

I meant what I'd said — I loved Annabelle but this relationship wasn't what either of us wanted any more. And while I was the one to initiate the breakup conversation, I knew deep down it was what she wanted too.

She deserved better than what we'd been giving each other lately. So did I.

We were going through the motions and staying together for the sake of being together—because it was comfortable and familiar. We'd barely spoken over the summer when I'd gone home to Portland and she'd gone home to California. And now that we were back at Pierson, things had been... *strained*.

"We've tried to make this work, Belle. You know we have..."

She stared back at me, her unreadable expression making me uneasy. I couldn't tell if she was going to burst into tears or send another projectile in my direction. I wanted to close the space between us and hold her, just like I'd always done whenever she was upset. But I knew that wouldn't work this time. It would only make things harder for both of us.

She shook her head. "I just never thought after everything we've been through that you'd dump me a month into your senior year. And two weeks before my birthday."

There was never a good time to break up with someone. But surely two weeks before her birthday was better than *on* her birthday?

Only I didn't have the balls to say that out loud. Not if I wanted to keep them attached to my body.

"Is there someone else?" she asked, voice quiet.

I softened. "No, there's no one else. We just can't pretend this is working anymore."

Wrong thing to say.

I knew it the second the words were out of my mouth.

Her face contorted with anger. "Pretend this is working? You're telling me you've been pretending with me?"

"No, that's not what I meant..." I took another placating step towards her.

"Get out, Adam. Just get the hell out."

She marched across the room and hauled the door open, watching my every step with a hardened expression.

I paused on my way out, my gaze locking with hers. "I really am sorry, Belle."

Her eyes pinched at the corners but she didn't respond and when I slipped into the hallway, she slammed the door behind me.

A gut-punching breakup definitely wasn't the way I'd planned to start my senior year.

Keeping my head down, I hustled down the steps of the residence hall and away from the girl I'd cared about for the past two years, whose heart I'd just ripped out, and lied to while doing it.

Because there was someone else.

And I couldn't stop thinking about her.

Only problem was, she wanted nothing to do with me.

Sign up for my newsletter to hear when the next book in the series will be released!

Or follow me on Instagram for all the latest news, book updates and giveaways.

Acknowledgments

So many people to thank. And so little space to do it in!

This kind of feels like that scene in Friends where Rachel and Phoebe pretend they're accepting an award at the Grammys while using Joey's Soapie trophy...

Firstly, I want to thank *you* for reading this book and taking a chance on a wide-eyed new author. I can't put into words the depth of my gratitude for helping me make my dreams come true and I hope you continue to come along for the ride.

To my husband and son, for their unwavering support, especially when whatever manuscript I'm working on never fails to steal so much of my attention. You're endlessly encouraging and I'm lucky I get to be your wife and mama.

To my parents, for not only being the best I could hope for, but for making sure my childhood was filled with books.

To my mother-in-law and sisters-in-law, thanks for entertaining my kiddo when I was in the thick of it, trying to get words on the page. It made all the difference.

To my speedy critique readers on this story— Steph, Mel, Liz — thank you for casting your critical and encouraging eyes over Monty and West's story and helping me make it what it is. I value your wisdom and words so much.

To my editor, Amy, for being so much fun as well as a talented editor!

Thank you to my 'Support Bras', Steph and Courtney. You've read every story, helped with every decision from plotting and titles to cover models and marketing, and cheered me on through every creative doubt. There's no one like you two and I'm lucky to call you friends.

To all my writer and reader friends, in real life and online, I'm so glad I get to be part of your circles.

Thanks for reading. 🖤

About the Author

Elouise Tynan is a young adult and new adult contemporary and fantasy romance author obsessed with stories about strong heroines and swoony heroes mixed with laughter, a whole lot o' love and a little bit of heat.

She lives in Melbourne, Australia with her husband and son.

Visit her at:
www.elouisetynan.com
Instagram: @elouisetynanwrites

Printed in Great Britain
by Amazon

74316870R00139